My grandchildren and great grandchildren:
And all those children who will never know the
'Good Years of Yesterday'.

Ivan Grosvenor Hawthorn

LIFE BEYOND TOMORROW

Austin Macauley Publishers®
LONDON · CAMBRIDGE · NEW YORK · SHARJAH

Copyright © Ivan Grosvenor Hawthorn 2025

The right of Ivan Grosvenor Hawthorn to be identified as author of this work has been asserted by him/her in accordance with sections 77 and 78 of the Copyright, Designs and Patents Act 1988.

All rights reserved. No part of this publication may be reproduced, stored in a retrieval system, or transmitted in any form or by any means, electronic, mechanical, photocopying, recording, or otherwise, without the prior permission of the publishers.

Any person who commits any unauthorized act in relation to this publication may be liable to criminal prosecution and civil claims for damages.

This is a work of fiction. Names, characters, businesses, places, events, locales, and incidents are either the products of the author's imagination or used in a fictitious manner. Any resemblance to actual persons, living or dead, or actual events is purely coincidental.

A CIP catalogue record for this title is available from the British Library.

ISBN 9781786930866 (Paperback)
ISBN 9781786296931 (Hardback)
ISBN 9781786296948 (ePub e-Book)

www.austinmacauley.com

First Published 2025
Austin Macauley Publishers Ltd®
1 Canada Square
Canary Wharf
London
E14 5AA

Summary
Life Beyond Tomorrow
(Fly cover)

One day whilst mowing the lawn, my faithful, old lawn mower, a Victa Mustang, coughed, banged, heaved a sigh and died a natural death. Being a mechanic of some note, I checked it out and found that it had stopped for the simple want of an ignition spark at the spark plug. In other words, it had no electricity. Fixing the fault, which was simply cleaning the oiled up, fouled spark plug, I restarted the mower and as I walked around and around in ever decreasing circles, mowing the lawn, I wondered, what would happen if the domestic and industrial supply of electricity was cut off and, in our lifetime, never came back on?

With this in mind, I finished the mowing, put the gardening tools and mower away and after washing my hands, sat down at my desk…and while the power was still on, switched on my faithful yet antique, 486 computer and after it eventually warmed up, wrote the following story, entitled: 'Life Beyond Tomorrow'.

Is it possible for someone to be like Galileo or Nostradamus and be able to see into the future without realising it, drought, global warming and empty water storages?

Written as a flight of fancy, 'Life Beyond Tomorrow' is simply a personal view of things to come…a turmoil of thoughts. A story, totally divorced from the tedium of everyday word-perfect scientific or factual writing, it was something that I found diverse, exciting, relaxing and easy to write. Yet in some ways, the outcome was frightfully thought provoking.

In writing 'Life Beyond Tomorrow', I simply let the mind wander…The pen flowed, the story materialised and without really evaluating or researching the subject or giving the consequences of my ramblings or predictions any thought, I simply wrote whatever came to mind. These thoughts recorded with tongue in cheek is about what we are doing to our planet. It tells of the lack of foresight by generations of politicians failing to predict the demands on every day vital services. An era of over-zealous greenies. Of do-gooders and robotic manufacturing. Computer wizardry along with the decline of human involvement in industry and in everyday life, until eventual reaching a point where the peak syndrome, had been achieved. Could the scientists of tomorrow have unwittingly created, worked towards and actually encouraged a natural disaster?

A disaster, that one-day, in the not-too-distant future, would culminate in the loss of a society and all the known services, which we know today. A way of life, now taken for granted, which could, and in fact did disappear instantly in a fiery atomic flash or any other man-made disaster. I wondered if this did happen; how would people survive? How, in the distant future would a thoroughly pampered populace adapt to a new and very hostile environment. An environment completely devoid of every day commodities; commodities that they had been brought up with, relied on and for generations, had simply taken for granted!

Strangely enough, within a year of committing these thoughts to paper in the form of a manuscript aptly entitled 'Life Beyond Tomorrow', in the January of 1998, the city of Auckland, New Zealand suffered a complete and utter devastating power failure. Then later in 1999, the metropolis of Sydney, Australia was left without power. In the August of 2003, 60% of America and most major Canadian cities on the 1 power grid were blacked out by a massive power failure, which the modern-day fail-safe computer system failed to arrest, causing the entire power grid to shut down.

In late August of 2003, the seething, ever moving Metropolis of London, UK, moving plus ten million commuters in and out of the city a day, suffered the same fate. In the September of 2003, the entire Chinese mainland suffered a complete and power devastating failure and with seconds, ground to a halt. During the recent cyclonic flooding in New Orleans, USA where many thousands trapped in offices and buildings as the city was left without power. The huge 7.8 earthquake that created havoc in Christchurch, New Zealand in 2010-11… In March of 2011, a huge 9.8 earthquake and the following tsunami which wreaked havoc on Northern Japan, the lack of electrical power to cool the rods, caused the Fukashima Daiichi atomic power generating plant to fail and virtually melt down. Thus, leaving the surviving millions in that region without power, and due to radiation fallout, creating food and water shortage. Finally, in October of 2014, super storm drenched the State of South

Australia leaving that state blacked out due to water infiltrating the electrical supply. Each nation mentioned was subjected to the very thing, I have dared to suggest in the coming pages, the loss of power.

Then the final straw that broke the camel's back… In Australia, in 2011, the incumbent labour party believing itself to be moving forward, introduced a carbon tax to control the emission output into the atmosphere from heavy industrial polluters. In the coming years, this action not only contributed to the closure of many of the countries coalmines and production industries, but to a change to the world climatic conditions.

Yes, it had all become a reality.

Without power, the cities mentioned had been plunged into industrial turmoil and financial chaos. When New Zealand was shut down electrically for a short four weeks; the business community suffered a conservative financial loss more than $350 million a day, so one can only hazard a guess at the loss suffered by the other major cities. However, that short power failure not only created temporary extreme hardship, bankruptcy and loss of livelihood for those in the various cities, but also further a field where the rural sector, was involved, both directly and indirectly. For the first time in their lives, the inhabitants were to experience an alien world, one without electricity and all the commodities and creature comforts that went with it.

Just think for a moment…What would happen if the power never went back on? Could the Australian, American, British, New Zealand, Chinese and now Japanese experience; be a timely warning…or simply an incredible coincidence?

I wonder.

Ivan G Hawthorn Esq. BEM. JP. ASA

The ANARE living quarters situated on the isthmus between North Head and the island proper. Lat 54°

Foreword

The year is 2150, the environmental green party controls the world, and the anti-pollution conservation groups, together combined with a worldwide trend to the electro/mechanical evolution, controlled the once lucky country of ours, Australia.

The peak syndrome, where the human race had become just another bystander, a product in the chain of this evolution, which was now, well and truly established. Australia, following a worldwide environmental trend; was just another country where audio-visual (A-V) communication systems, robotics and computerisation had been so effectively utilised and harnessed in recent times, had taken over the day-to-day routine existence of industrial labour and mundane domestic management. Moreover, as multi-lingual, audio-visual systems had long since taken over communications, very few people could now read and certainly few could or were required to write.

2150, an era in which everything was simply taken for granted, it was a whole new and exciting world of electronics where neither mind nor body was involved in tiring routine work or thought. It was a world, where for the majority at least, a different machine, via though transference or a simple voice activated command, catered for every need. Over the past two centuries and certainly without realising it, the inhabitants of this once lucky country had by their own design, become vegetables. Very high-class vegetables, but vegetables nevertheless. Totally reliant on Electro Magnetic Forces (EMF), which virtually controlled and, in fact, dominated their lives.

This was a world where the environmentalist and eco-groups had achieved virtual power and the world was once more a vast green belt. Large areas of rain forests and almost impenetrable jungles covered most reaches of Australian and in fact the world once more. To remove any living plant, tree or shrub or to walk upon the grass was like treason a crime against the state. It was a land where the inhabitants now lived in isolation, virtual prisoners beneath a lush canopy of vegetation. It was an area where emission control and carbon taxing wrought havoc on the inhabitants. Through this man-made canopy, the sun rarely shone and humidity was incredibly high. Because of the constant high humidity, rainfall over the centuries had increased ten-fold.

Like the rest of the world, Australia had embraced the worldwide trend – the innovation and utilisation of computerised, robotic manufacturing and domestic cyborg servants. It was a world where every process was a function of computerised programming or manufacturing. In factories, cyborgs, almost human in their functions and appearance, fitted, removed and reset production tools when worn or broken. These machines also controlled the manufacturing, removal and storage of finished components. In hospitals and surgeries, where computerised diagnosis and operating equipment took their place, surgeons and family doctors, simply became observers.

Moving walkways or people movers transported the crowds within the sealed shopping complexes, social venues and spaceports. While in most homes, pre-programmed domestic appliances and cyborg servants were also utilised. These were homes where domestic and routine chores were achieved without the need of anyone to afford even the slightest thought as to how they were achieved.

Because of this industrial electronic-revolution, two thirds of the nation's work force was now redundant, replaced by these highly intelligent and more productive machines. These machines were not paid, they did not stop to sleep or to eat and when worn out, were simply discarded and replaced by another. Therefore, commodities continued to flow endlessly from the various production lines. The price of this transition to a maximum productivity output was as the sale of goods decreased a financial and economic disaster.

"Why?" Simple, because the people that once made those commodities were now un-employed and did not have the money or a credit status to buy the robotic made vehicles, machinery and everyday household commodities.

The politicians and the higher echelon of society seemed oblivious to the fact that day in and day out, the machines continued manufacturing and spewing out commodities. The result of so few people being employed was that, warehouses became full of un-sold goods and superseded, anti-gravitational transport units filled the warehouses. Storage yards were now full of new or superseded equipment, which would never be sold.

Once more, the world was divided into several classes. At the top of the chain, the very rich, wanting for nothing. Then the blue-collar worker, the scientists and electronic specialists, the white-collar businessperson and his employees. Then, the unemployed and the redundant; the latter, as superannuating payouts quickly disappeared, were slowly but surely eating themselves out of existence. Another group hidden away in homes and hospices were the elderly, the conveniently forgotten senior generation, living on the memories of a world that used to be and dam little else.

Finally, the ferals, the forgotten people of the forest. These were a community of former everyday working-class families, now nomadic dwellers of the forest. People that had long since shunned this new style of civilisation for one of Mother Nature.

Day after day, month after month, year after year, the electronic wizards and the computer orientated scientists of the 22nd century, slowly but surely converted everyday occupations into a system of automation. Places of work, shopping, banking, physical and mechanical transportation had all become a system of electronic wizardry. Indeed, an electronic evolution, one that had now reached its peak and humanity had simply become a passenger…a by-product.

For those perched precariously on the top of the financial chain, life was one idyllic day after another with nothing to do except enjoy the freedom from repetitive chores. However, for the forgotten majority at the other end of the social scale, life had not changed all that much. The equipment and the necessities for a good life were there, but for most, it was well beyond their capacity to purchase, re-stock or maintain. Life for those caught up in this now, electronically controlled world, proceeded as it had over the last one-point five centuries. Only now, except when in transit, they were virtual prisoners, confined to their own homes and with each passing day, the chance of any improvement in the near future being remote. The scene can be generalised through the eyes of just one family whose story runs parallel to most of the world's inhabitants. In this case, a family living in the once sprawling City of Greater Geelong in the State of Victoria, Australia. The only difference being that, when crunch came, the lights went out and this ideal world came crashing down around them was that, this family was prepared to do something about their situation.

Chapter 1
Macquarie Island

Picture an aerial shot of an approaching island, some twenty-five miles long, from the southern end, north to what is known as North Head at its most northerly point. It is a large, lush green yet totally barren treeless island known as Macquarie Island. Originally discovered in 1810 by Captain Hasselburough, Master of a Brigantine; rigged sailing vessel 'The Perseverance'. Macquarie Island is the last bastion or landmass between Australia and the cold, bleak, ice-covered continent of Antarctica.

The passing panorama shows many small settlements scattered along the eastern coastline, namely Hurd point, Lusitanian Bay, Green Gorge, Sandy Bay and the Nuggets along and finally the main living quarters or settlement under North Head. Coming and going in view, it shows the many small stone huts, which are used by shepherds, tending the numerous flocks of sheep, herds of goats and red deer, which can be seen grazing contentedly in the many protected, hidden valleys such as the Red River valley area or along the steep sheltered slopes of the eastern coastline.

The many indigenous species, such as southern elephants and seals are seen by the thousands; sleeping or moulting along the shoreline in great slothful heaps, or they would be beach masters engaged in aggressive territorial battles, battles for the control of hereditary harems, which are situated on and along both sides of the northern isthmus. Also, the abundance of Fur Seals on the many rocky escarpments on and around the base of Hurd Point to the south and on North Head to the north.

In the many large rookeries, some covering an area of up to 14½ acres, are four species of penguins, going about their annual breeding cycle: these are the king penguin, the royal penguin, the rockhopper and the gentoo penguin.

Also, there are four various species of Albatross on their solitary mud and grass, truncated shaped nests and Dominican gulls, skuas and ground nesting or burrowing Petrels of all kinds, some of which were now in flight. In addition, created by the wild, turbulent seas of the 'Furious Fifties', which crashed continuously along the entire length of its rocky western foreshore, sense the anger that is Macquarie Island. Finally, focus on the small plateau on top of North Head, where we see a small group of children dressed in an ill assortment of warm homemade, windproof yet presentable sheepskin and leather clothing stand clustered about an elderly man.

It is now the middle of the 22nd century, and this small group standing beneath a solitary, slowly spinning wind generator, perched high on the western lip of North Head, are gathered in front of a small cemetery surrounded by a weathered, white-painted picket fence. In this small cemetery, not only the original deceased inhabitants of this new and isolated colony lay at rest, but also some deceased members of various Australian National Antarctic Research

Expeditions that once wintered here. Expeditioner's, that had lived and died here while conducting scientific duties a long…long time ago.

Here in this same, small well-cared-for cemetery are the graves of their own immediate past families, also relatives and friends who made that original perilous journey to freedom during the 21st century. The ANARE people (Australian National Antarctic Research Expedition members) also buried here were from a much earlier occupation of the island. Some of whom were friends of the great-great grandfather of this small group when he was once the leader of two such scientific expeditions – and now lies buried here beside some of his men.

Looking out over the wild, restless South Pacific Ocean, the old man gazed longingly towards the Northern Hemisphere, where now a century on, somewhere out there, a far different civilisation was once again rising from the ashes.

Yes…somewhere out there a thousand miles or more in any direction, a civilisation far different from this one was slowly rising out of the decay and radioactive waste. Recent feeble, yet garbled radio signals indicated that some sort of transmission from the world, his ancestors once knew, was now possible. Yet, here on this island, with all the sophisticated equipment at their disposal and a carrier signal being transmitted at regular intervals, they had not been able to lock on to anyone.

Today was Sunday and as there was no school, down below the steep southern wall of North Head; several older children were playing cricket on the large communal square situated amongst the cluster of small yet brightly painted buildings on the northern extremity of a narrow, sandy isthmus.

This small satellite community, isolated by a strong rock wall from the many thousands of elephant seals, which annually come ashore to breed along the sandy isthmus, is similar in design but on a much larger scale, than the other five communities, strategically located about the island.

The other living quarters situated around the island are located primarily on the eastern side of the island at Sandy Bay, Green Gorge, Lusitania Bay and at Hurd Point on far the southeastern end of the island. While on the western side, about one-third of the way down the coastline and situated at the back of a vast open, windswept beach is the smaller resort complex of Bauer Bay. As a rule, some of the older residents use Bauer Bay for R&R in the spring and summer time as a vacation resort or when things get too much for them and finally as a honeymoon retreat. Finally, yet most importantly is the large living complex at Caroline Cove, situated in the shadow of Petrel Peak on the far southwestern corner of the island. The rest of the island and its plateau are as it has always been wet, wild, windswept and unpolluted by humans.

With the cessation of sealing and penguining for skins and oil in 1919, the island was formally declared a wild life sanctuary in 1933. The endemic species of fauna and flora are now living and breeding undisturbed on traditional sites, as they did throughout the ages, have once more, regained something of their former numbers.

Up above the indigenous fauna, (seals and penguins) which due to the extreme climatic conditions and geologic structure of the island can only live and breed for a few months of the year on a few accessible areas. These are to be found around the base of the island at sea level. The community's own small flocks of sheep, goats and red deer, live and breed in the many hidden, well-protected and secluded valleys situated along the eastern wall of the island.

Alternatively, on what is locally known as the Amphitheatre, which is an undulating, grassy area situated high above Caroline Cove near Waterfall Lake on the southwestern shoulder of the island. Also in the Red River area, again situated in a deep, protected valley on the eastern side of the island between Sandy Bay and Green Gorge. Finally, grazed on the extreme southern end of the island between Hurd Point and Caroline Cove, where they ranged free on a broad protected terrace or ledge situated above the steep cliffs and immediately below the southern end of the plateau.

There during the warmer seasons, contained behind primitive, dry stone fences or corrals, which had been constructed over the years the various species are allowed to graze and multiply; undisturbed in these protected areas until required as a source of food or for the wool or the hair they produced. These by-products were used to make knitted garments and finally slaughtered not only for food but also for their hides and skins, which were used in the manufacture of clothing, footwear and other leather items.

These domestic flocks were watched over during the short spring and summer, by rotating families of shepherds who lived out an idyllic yet hermit like existence in one of the many quaint, little, mud and grass insulated stone cottages, which are situated at each of these grazing sites. The stones used in the construction of these small cottages and the 18th century, convict-styled, dry-stone fences, were carried up from the nearby seashore by people travelling up and down the island. Over the years, many hundreds of tons of stone had been manually transported up into these farming communities; where on arrival, they were placed on the fence line or simply left at the building site as they passed.

During the late autumn, in readiness for the coming onslaught of winter, the stock is moved down from the steep eastern slopes and lower plateau regions, which would soon be subjected to the semi-darkness, the cold, icy westerly winds and the blinding snow storms of the long, dark Sub-Antarctic winter's night. The various flocks are protected from winter's severe climate in stone corrals or housed under roofed shelters, situated along the protected eastern side of the island, where they stood a better chance of survival than if left to the elements.

At each of the six smaller communities, a small controlled herd of sheep and deer were kept for consumption along with a few goats for milk. After milking each morning, it was the responsibility of older children to herd the flocks up along the slopes of the surrounding hillsides in their immediate area to feed on the abundance of cabbage weed, tussock grass and the many varieties of ferns and watercress. Where possible, the animals were kept away from the pleurophylum and other rare endemic native grasses – this was one chore which was sometimes rather hard to police.

Since their arrival on the island many years before, the new settlers had maintained the former station scientifically, resurrected and continued the original major scientific studies. In fact, there was little that the new inhabitants did not know or record about the island or its endemic inhabitants.

Today the group of children being chaperoned along the windy, exposed top of North Head by their granddad, stopped to look out over the endless moving sea.

"Granddad," one of the little girls enquired as she tightly squeezed the old man's hand… "What is out there beyond the sea, is there really other people and children like us?"

"Yes, my child, there certainly is, or rather there was when your ancestors left their homes," her grandfather replied and continued, "When I was no bigger than you, there was a vast, modern, highly sophisticated and intelligent race of human beings out there in a world, electronically and climatically far different to what we know here."

"Why! They even put men on the moon, had manned orbiting space stations and had travelled as far away as Mars and Jupiter and the 'Voyager' space probe which disintegrated in deep space away back as far as the 22nd of September, 2003 after a flight lasting almost a quarter of a century."

"Unfortunately," he said, "Slowly but surely the electronic age of computer wizardry, digital electronics, anti-gravitational transport, voice recognition robots and equipment peaked and the population became victims of its own making. Green society parties, environmental lobby groups of the day and those caught up in a dream to save the world environmentally, pushed through policies and legislation to protect and preserve the environment for the children of tomorrow. In fact, it was this same legislation that was to be their down fall."

"You see the generators down there," he said, pointing to the building, housing three diesel-powered engines creating the power supply. "Well, sadly equipment like that was banned back in 2030 in the so-called civilised world."

"Why?" asked an incredulous youngster.

"Because they emit carbon dioxide and other toxic emissions. Anything emitting carbon dioxide was banned by the middle of the last century because it was supposedly responsible for heating up the atmosphere."

"What about the big power grid in that place in central Australia?" asked another. "I've forgotten the name of the city…but I've heard that it was where all the electronic power induction cells for the whole country were generated."

"Fink," said the old man. "Ah, yes…that place out there used to be a desert, believe it or not…you wouldn't think so now…have you ever seen pictures of the way it used to look?" He continued without waiting for an answer. "No one had ever heard of Fink until the whole idea of nuclear generation, fragmenting matter, instantly transporting it and materialising at its destination, anti-gravitational transport system that fragments matter and re-materialises it, was invented."

"Well, meant by-laws which were designed to protect the environment, somehow backfired, as did the introduced laws protecting all living things. All emissions were banned and in a few short years, Mother Nature took over, once more, creating vast, primeval rain forests."

"Finally, the humidity created beneath the vast, green canopy, a canopy, which now covered the land, was such, that beneath it, rain fell continuously."

"Well…one day, the water found its way into the main atomic power generation system, which caused a short circuit in the cooling system, this caused the nuclear rods to melt down and the power house simply exploded. Now without power there was nothing to support life as the people knew it."

"So, our grandparents, or your great grandparents and their friends, actually some of the people we come up here to visit," he said, pointing to the neat, little graveyard surrounded by a badly flaking, white-painted picket fence, "decided to leave Australia and return to a normal way of life and a family existence."

"If you would all like to come over here and sit in the protection of the tall tussock grass out of the wind," the old man said, moving over to the eastern edge of the plateau. "I will tell you the story," he continued with a chuckle, "as a matter of fact, I may write a book about it one day. But then again." He laughed. "There is no one to publish or to read it, is there?"

There, accompanied by the murmur of the warm spring wind, known affectionately as the 'Snow Fairy', the lonely cry of the sea birds, the Dominican gulls; the McCormack and great southern skuas now riding the wind currents and eddies along the cliff faces or the foreshore far below. Along with the busy rasping, rustling sound of the ever-present westerly wind, as it ran quickly through the tall fields of moving, waving tussock grass. The voice of their grandfather carried on the morning wind, drifted out over the lonely expanse of the cold, grey Southern Ocean as though searching, reaching back in time, as he probed his mind for an era long past; a shadowy, fleeting memory of a civilisation, now long past and virtually extinct. Finally, he related to them an incredible story, a story that seemed to their innocent, inquiring young minds, almost too unbelievable to be true. Yet, even to the smallest detail, it was so very true.

Chapter 2
The Wedding Day

"A long, long time ago, somewhere to the north over the horizon there," Granddad said, gesturing north beyond Bishop and Clarke Islands with a gnarled finger. "Our ancestors once lived in the City of Greater Geelong. This city, nestling on the shimmering shores of Corio Bay in the State of Victoria, was a vast sprawling city of a quarter of a million people, a proud and beautiful provincial city, in a vast, lucky country, known as Australia.

"Situated at 30°10' south latitude and 144°24' east longitude, its site was first viewed from station peak in the You Yangs, a mountain range consisting of Anyaghe Yousang (meaning two hills) and Wurdi Yousang (Big Hill) some 16 miles NNW of Geelong in 1802, discovered by Hume and Hovel in 1824.

"Laid out by Sir Robert Bourke, then Governor of NSW during his visit to the area in 1837, coincidentally the same year that Melbourne and Williamstown, far across Port Phillip Bay, were established. Geelong was a thriving colony, producing commodities such as wheat, cattle, gold, wool, fruit, potatoes, grapes-wine, making stud and draft horses. Also, on the banks of the Moorabool River created/designed the first refrigeration plant, which now stands in the Smithsonian institute museum in the USA. Geelong with a thriving export port, conveyed commodities to countries around the world. It also ran a paddle steamer ferry across the bay to Melbourne.

"Over the coming centuries, with a population now exceeding 300,000, Geelong grew into an important cultural and trading centre; the once small colony expanded into a beautiful, exciting city with many prominent buildings made of local blue stone and sand stone, churches of all denomination and a Catholic Basilica. It boasted a Botanical Garden of 200 acres and Johnston Park Garden of 2 ½ acres in the city centre created by Governor Latrobe.

"God…how things changed in just a few generations."

"Well," he continued, "way back in 21st century, 2050 in fact; the world was quickly heading towards a social and mechanical controlled state of total confusion. The green power activists and environmental ideology groups were in office, supposedly governing the country, industry and society alike. Any contrivances giving off carbon emissions were banned. Along the way, to improve the atmosphere, they had introduced an anti-gravitational pollution free transportation system. One that whistled silently by on a beamed power source, as well as other non-pollutant units or controlled beam rider systems powered by electronic induction power cells relying on a major 'EMF' (1) output signal beamed from the remote 'National Central Power Grid' which was situated in 'Fink' a small isolated township in far north of South Australia. This grid was one of only three such powerhouses in the world.

"For daily commuting, people, goods and materials were fragmented and transferred electronically from one point to another. Air from factories and industrial plants was recycled and bubbled up filtered through large man-made lakes, which dominated the landscape. Naturally, these lakes were out of bounds, humans were not permitted to swim in or to use them for any recreational purpose. All over and about the city VFT gravity services and interplanetary spacecraft moved silently by on pollution-free anti-gravitational drive systems, while out on Corio Bay, marine service appliances hovered silently above the holding pens of a large, aquatic fish farm.

"To replace the currency known by their fore fathers, a completely new world of EFTPOS or a consumer credit system complete with computer home banking credit transfers, evolved. There was however, one small yet very important factor in these idyllic life styles that the modern designers had overlooked… Mother Nature. Yes… Mother Nature.

(*1) Electro Magnetic Force)

"Why worry about nature you might ask? We can control it, they said. From the east, the sun even though you could not see, for the cloud cover had always risen in the morning, shone down on the earth throughout the day, and eventually set in the west. The flora and fauna of the earth was no longer taken for granted, it was nurtured, pampered and protected. As were the birds of the air and the fishes of the sea, and every animal that inhabited the land. Yes, the children of Mother Nature were always there. Besides, the modern-day electronic genius and the computer-orientated inventors were simply far too busy fussing over their creative computers, to worry about the bloody weather.

"Unfortunately, a century later…in 2149, the rain, with no El Nino or La Nina to contend with, continued to fall as it had throughout recorded modern history, but over the last half century it was more continuous than ever before. Day after day, month in and month out, it had fallen steadily. The vast network of now unused national highways, which cut an ugly swathe through the countryside, like bulging veins on a dying planet were simply awash. Moreover, as each month passed, they looked more like endless rivers than the once modern highways and freeways. Thousands of banned, non-conforming vehicles waiting recycling simply floated about their water-logged storage yards. While outside the sealed homes or the work places, life that had already started to slow down, eventually stopped.

"As the rain continued, 2150 dawned wet and humid. Across the land, water levels continued to rise at an alarming rate and the country became one giant wetland. Never before had you seen so many happy ducks, swans and waterfowl, cranes and geese. Crocodiles now infested waters where they had never been seen before. Now an everyday occurrence, rivers ran at an all-time high, breaking their banks and once losing their defined boundaries, quickly flooded any low-lying area; towns and inland cities, and like lake Eyre once a barren, dry Salt Lake, once more became vast inland sea.

"At the township of Alice Springs, situated in the very centre of Australia, as the Todd River flooded and once more rose to become a regular watercourse. The local aboriginal tribe, namely the 'Arrernti', which once numbered 21,481, had for centuries, been the only inhabitants of this once dry, sandy riverbed, were now forced to move to higher ground and make way for the torrents of water and the original inhabitants. As carried in the turbulent rushing waters, redfin, catfish, bream, carp, long-necked turtles and yabbies once more returned to feed along the river bottom. Ultimately, as the water continued to take over the centre of the continent, nothing was safe. It invaded everything: homes, shops, industrial sites and eventually a few hundred miles down the track in the state of South Australia…the township of Fink.

"The township of 'Fink', situated in the once dry, remote arid desert region of Northern South Australia, was home to the boffins, staff and families who maintained and operate Australia's one and only massive atomic power generation system. A system, which contributed not only for Australia's power demands, but was also part of a global 'Worldwide Power Generation system and Distribution Grid' supplying 50% of the world's power requirements.

"The Mary Kathleen mine had flooded and the supply of raw uranium or yellow cake required for the production of atomic fuel rods, ceased. Across central Australia, as the water slowly rose up over levee walls, and Lake Eyre once more became an inland sea, discharging billions of gallons over the countryside, finally reaching Fink. As the huge water pumps recently installed to safeguard this area from flooding, failed to cope with the rising volume of water, defying all attempts to prevent it from entering the power generation system…eventually did!

"Short-circuiting all internal electrical equipment including the electric motors that controlled the water pumps that were used to cool the reactor fuel rods. Without cooling, the reactor over heated; started a meltdown, creating a series of hydrogen explosions, which in turn as the two other overseas systems on the grid failed to cope with and carry the extra load, led to a chain reaction of explosions and power failures across the world.

"The explosion at the 'Fink' atomic power plant was a catastrophe of monumental proportions and as the resultant, atomic mushroom cloud billowed skyward, it signalled the end of an era. Radioactive debris and the resultant acid rain, carried on the prevailing northerly wind, rained down across the land. Around Australia and in fact the world, as one after another heavily over-loaded electronic system collapsed and failed, a world once totally supported by and reliant on electrical power for the wizardry of the 21st century, ground to a halt. Subsequently in the now heavily overloaded distribution centres, fires broke out across the great metropolises and cities of the world.

"Computerised and anti-gravitational cells reliant on the externally beamed energy source for power to support all forms of transportation, deep-sea farming communities, spacecraft and large international freight carriers, simply failed. Moreover, as the electronic impulse feeder system crashed, so did they; spiralling down into the bays or far out to sea, into cities and the countryside alike. While far out in deep space, inter-galactic passenger carrying spaceships and general cargo carriers, manned or un-manned planetary probes simply continued out into the endless reaches of the universe.

"Fragmented travellers commuting in personal projection systems (2Ps) simply vanished. Parents now trapped within their homes, frantically searched the flickering, dying instrument panels for signs of returning schoolchildren, which should have been arriving home about now on non-existent systems. However, sadly, they were all gone, never to return.

"By the end of that first horrific day, as commodity scanners failed to operate the inhabitants of the great cities of the world could not purchase food or supplies simply because the electronic tills using EFTPOS were now useless. Therefore, as there was no real legal tender, it did not really matter whether the check-out chick could add up or not. Shoppers and shop assistants alike, were now trapped inside giant mega-marts or departmental stores. In elevators and on escalators or moving internal footpaths. Those trapped inside the high-rise skyscrapers, in underground transportation chutes, office blocks and stores could not get out, and those outside could not get in. For without power to activate them, the electronically operated, armour-plated doors simply refused to open.

"Meanwhile, in their darkened laboratories, the scientists and technician who had inadvertently created this catastrophe, tried to come to terms with the terrible reality of their handy work, but they too were now trapped, victims of their own making. Without power to see by or to run their computers and digital analyser systems, they were useless. As they had never been taught to think for themselves and now without power to read their ID cards to activate the locked laboratory or office door, they too would now die here, simply because they could not get out.

"In Australia, as the city of Geelong slowly sank into its first night without power, all known support services had ground to a halt and with no firefighting service, vast sections of the city, now, burnt out of control. Instead of the organised tranquillity of living with nature, pandemonium and fear now reigned supreme. The inhabitants of the central city trapped in their darkened apartments and places of work, or homes that had now become instant prisons, wandered about in what can only be described as total confusion. Those that defied the law for what it was and had somehow smashed their way out of their homes, now searched for food ransacking outlets or distribution systems where they took the last of the prepared foods. As a direct result of that fiery atomic flash, there were no communications, no TV, no radio, no computers, no DVDs nor Internet.

"As there was no way of getting the food out, heating or cooking it, prepared foods in the refrigerated, automatic food dispensers, started to thaw. Most of the inhabitants of this magnificent, green futuristic city did not possess any cooking utensils or those that kept them only as antiques had long since forgotten how to use them. Worse still, for a century or more, as even life's most basic tasks had been done for them, the new generations had no idea of how to look after themselves. The result was universal mayhem.

"Our story began one day back in 2149, gala day, I think it was," their granddad said, "a day when most of Geelong's inhabitants were in the city centre attending the annual presentation of the 'National Green Shield Award', awarded nationally for outstanding achievements in the field of environmental protection; this prestigious shield was a vigorously contested trophy. This presentation had long since taken the place of 'Gala Day', a day when gaily decorated floats once paraded through the city streets. A day of football finals and Sheffield shield cricket matches. Geelong Gala Day also supported many carnivals, as well as arts and craft stalls; all displayed in colourful, open-air markets and fairs, which were the hallmark of gala day. However, they do not exist anymore."

"You know why?"

"Well, it was because a jungle-like rainforest had long since taken over our once bustling thriving city and there were in fact no streets for the floats to parade down any more. Gone was the parks, grassed lawn area of Steam packet or Transvaal Square waterfront reserves to host the stalls.

"Yes… I remember that day as if it was only yesterday," the storyteller murmured. "Why even today, I can still hear the boring voice of the Lord Mayor."

"'And now ladies and Gentlemen to end the day's festivities,' the mayor of Geelong announced in a loud pretentious manner. 'It gives me great pleasure to announce that, for the third successive decade, our proud City of Greater Geelong has been awarded the 'Green Shield' by the National Conservation and Environment Committee.'"

"Almost drowned out by the constant rumble of thunder and the sharp, whip-cracking sound of the ever-present lightning flashes, a synthetic yet tumultuous rumble of applause could be clearly heard, even inside the sealed confines of their anti-gravitational vehicle (AGV). Inside the vehicle, Tim Hawthorn's lovely daughter, Deidre Ann, leant forward…hugged her mother, she whispered urgently, 'I do wish he would declare the festival closed, I have so much to do at home.'"

"'Tomorrow, will come soon enough,' her mum reassured her, 'your wedding day will be just perfect, your father and I have everything organised so don't you worry your pretty, little head about a thing.'"

"Although, her mother suggested, 'looking up towards the heavy canopy of foliage and the steadily rain falling, 'I do wish the rain would stop for just a little while, just one day without rain would be lovely!'"

"The festivities finally over, the assembly of AGV's, hovering silently above the city quickly dispersed into the surrounding suburbs, which with their lush covering of green vegetation looked more like the floor of an Amazon rainforest than a once thriving, prosperous inner city or suburban area. Today, beneath the thick canopy of trees, shrubs and tenacious ivy, lantana and other species of clinging vines; which had long since covered not only the houses, but outbuildings, fences and playing fields as well, from the air, most homes were no longer visible.

"'One of these days,' Tim said, almost absent-mindedly to his wife, 'those blasted greenies are going to wake up to themselves and realise that human beings have to live on this planet as well.'"

"'Ssssshhh, for goodness sake,' Margaret whispered, 'someone might report you, and that's all we'd need.'"

"'It's bloody true though,' Tim mumbled. 'Those idiots in their laboratories and ivory towers can't see the forest for the trees.'

"'With all this vegetation, the humidity and the excess oxygen has converted this once semi-dry country of ours into a blasted rainforest, that's why the rain has been so constant over the last few decades.' 'And besides,' he added, 'I wish someone would hear I'm bloody fed up with it.'"

"As he programmed the LGS (location guidance system) on board, their AGV to guide them home, the steadily falling rain, as it swirled across the decaying city, created crazy, bizarre patterns on the canopy of their old AGV. As he moved the thrust potentiometer forward to silently glided up out of the City Square, Tim felt that if it were not for the in-built LGS, even he would be battling to find his way home. A home, that was hidden somewhere down there beneath a thick ground covering of lush green vegetation, and invisible from the air or in fact anywhere!

"Tim felt that one day their aging AGV, even with all its updated technical modifications would not make it home. Yes, their faithful old Ford built AGV was due for an upgrade and as though everyone else was thinking the same, he suggested, 'You know, if I can get a consumer purchase credit upgrade at work tomorrow, I will trade the old Ford in for one of those new IDUs (Instant Destination Units), which will not only save time, but would also put on a bit of a show for the guests at the wedding tomorrow.'"

"Abruptly cutting through his train of thoughts, Margaret added coldly, 'And before the guests arrive, you might also clear out that pile of ancient mechanical junk, which you have had housed in the shed all these years.'

"'It's no good,' she continued. 'No one in their right mind is interested in all that rusty, old junk or antique equipment, as you call it, any more…tell me, go on, tell me?' she taunted. 'How long is it since a paying customer came to look at it? Don't worry I will tell you, it has been years…hasn't it.'"

"Tim was hurt, it might be a lot of junk to her and all the other blasted greenies, but not to him. The many different makes and models of heavy, World War 2 Military vehicles, amphibians, classic motor bikes and various marques of vintage Jaguar cars, along with assorted power generators and mechanical tools of trade were all that he had to remind him of a vibrant era, now past.

"An era, when his father and grandfather had driven and maintained such unique vehicles with great pride. A time when interstate highways and broad freeways and autobahns were still open and they had travelled to the many popular racing circuits, which then existed around the countryside. Circuits, where on most weekends, he had thrilled to the sound of the high-powered racing cars, the throbbing noise of their powerful engines, which filled the air with an ear shattering, throaty roar as he revelled in the heady aroma of high octane-nitro fuel and paraffin oil. That was of course, before they and lot of other machinery powered by fossil fuel were banned because of their so-called toxic carbon emissions. Emissions that were supposedly breaking down the O3 in the ozone layer.

"Bloody rubbish! It was their upper atmospheric atomic bomb test. Deliberately lit oil fires during the wars in Kuwait and Iraq, the soot and carbon given off from burning oil wells during the Gulf war some year's prior and years of bush fires in California, Australia, Burma and the surrounding Indonesian islands. Fires, which had generated enough carbon and heat to break down the O3 or ozone layer for generations to come that had done the damage, not the poor, old motor car.

"Tim often wondered what the authorities would do if it ever became known that he still had a vast quantity of fossil fuel, diesel and petrol stashed away in large underground tanks buried deep beneath the workshop floor to power this collection. Fuel tanks coupled to a series of innocent-looking display fittings and a pump with a vapour sensor, wired in reverse, so it indicated zero toxic vapour. As long as he did not break the seals, put there by the inspectors years ago or take the vehicles out of the display shed, they were safe.

"As dusk fell on what was to be the final Gala Day, the rain, as though it knew, controlled the lives of all those hidden away beneath the canopy, gleefully blew and swirled merrily in and out of the forest, creating bizarre apparition and designs as it swirled in and out of its ghostly surroundings. Nowadays, as the burning of wood or any other natural fossil fuel was strictly forbidden. Smoke no longer rose lazily from the many elaborate yet disused chimneys, which were now home to a multitude of birds and opossum. Likewise, that tantalising, long-forgotten aroma, which conjured up the memories of many; a cosy night cuddled up with a loved one in front of an open fire with hot, buttered toast and thick pea soup followed by toasted marshmallows. While from somewhere in the background, the romantic sound of music from an old 45-rpm record player softly muffled with a recently removed ladies stocking, now stuffed in the speaker horn to diffuse the sound, romantically filling the room.

"Today the sound was vastly different, as the impersonal sound of digital auto-entertainment systems, spewed forth a loud raucous noise from the entertainment, consoles something called music (for the want of a name), but it was nothing like the sounds of yesteryear. While at the same time, unseen light density systems regulated the interior of the house to brighten or dimmed the lights to keep it in harmony with the sound or the mood.

"On their arrival home, the day of the presentation, the AGV hovered momentarily above their dwelling, and taking the vines and creepers with it, a reception chute in the roof slid opened. Then, riding a guidance beam the AGV automatically descending into the transportation port. Safely housed, the roof section slide silently closed as Tim shut the vehicle down. Raising the canopy, the family were quick to vacate the vehicle and disperse throughout the house. Margaret, by simply pressing the appropriate selection codes to program and combined the evening meal, busied herself preparing an early dinner from a wide selection of meat, vegetarian or seafood meals available in the auto-food dispenser. Once selected, the meals were automatically pre-programmed for serving at the correct serving temperature by the bar code on them in an integrated internal microwave system. The exception of course being salads and other cold dishes.

"As tomorrow's wedding demanded that everyone be out of bed, bright and early, following dinner that evening, it was off to bed early. Tomorrow, there were a hundred and one things to do. The women had their hair appointments, the caterers would be in, setting up the wedding breakfast and the marriage celebrant had to be transferred to the house. The bridal bouquets and flowers, pre-ordered with permission obtained from the state-regulated forest and floral department had to be collected and signed for. So many things, which required doing at the last moment, meant that there would be no time for anyone to sleep in.

"The following morning, music from the audio/visual entertainment, console rudely, disturbed the sleeping household to yet another wet, misty grey dawn and on a pre-programmed circuit, the auto-domestic cyborg servants commenced their cleaning cycle. Robotic maid's carried out a linen exchange, vacuumed the house and dispensed an instant pre-packaged breakfast. When breakfast was finished the utensils used were automatically whisked away and cleaned, and by 8 am, the house was clean, almost to a point of being sterile, as well as virtually deserted.

"At this point in time, it would seem that apart from the wedding, there was nothing special about the day which was about to unfold. A day, in which life, as the family and indeed the world once knew, would never be the same again.

"Stepping into the 2P (Personal-Projector), Tim entered his destination code, de-materialised and departed for work. During the day, he would check on the credit status and try for an upgrade, then look into the possibility of the AGV upgrade. On his departure, Deidre, on re-programming the 2P, disappeared, en-route to the dressmaker for the final fitting and later to return with her wedding suit, followed him closely.

In this modern era due to the much-publicised depletion of the ozone layer (O_3) and the reputed high intensity of the Ultraviolet radiation over the last five to six decades, pretty dresses or frilly open-necked blouses which showed the occasional glimpse of a creamy white bosom. Tomboy-like jeans and baggy shirts tied around the waist with an old tie, along with dad's old, heavy working boots as footwear were unknown today… In fact, as they were a thing of the past. Today, worn outside the protection of the home or workplace where people seldom ventured anyhow or in anti-gravitational vehicles, a reflective metallic like UV resistant silver material, which shielded the wearer from the supposedly harmful rays, was now used to make semi-spacesuit-like clothing.

Today, in comparison to the yards and yards of lace, silk and taffeta or tulle of yester-year or simple cotton prints, which were once used in the production of feminine clothing, how strange this new apparel looked. The beautiful wedding gowns with long flowing trains and tulle veils that her mother and grandmother and other female relatives, now long since passed away, would have once worn, were but a pictorial memory. Alternatively, simple, loose cotton prints worn during those heady, romantic days of summer and picnics by the sea, or cuddled up in the back seat of a convertible at a drive-in theatre, where most wanted or unwanted children were conceived, were to the older members of the family, just a memory but to the modern generation, simply unknown.

"As the morning progressed, Wayne, the prospective bridegroom, employed out on the state-owned, commercial aquatic fish farm in Corio Bay, had been un-expectedly called in to check on some communication problems, which had arisen in the control centre and as the rain intensified he worked on quite unconcerned.

"'Yep' it certainly looked as though it was going to be an inside wedding. While the bridal party would certainly object, out here on the bay, exposed to the constant rain and the elements all year round, Wayne was used to it and certainly would not worry about getting a bit wet. He and Deidre had met on a modern version of chat line and had by just conversing on a broad audio-visual screen, over the last few years, became romantically involved. As they always commuted fragmented, one-on-one time spent together was limited to the occasional visit to her home, a home that he had never seen from the outside.

"Meanwhile, back at the farm. Oops, sorry!

"Meanwhile, back at Tim's house, *'Beep, beep, beep'*, the activity alarm on the 2P announced the arrival of resident of the house or that of an incoming visitor. As Tim was certainly not due home for hours yet and Deidre would not have had time to even try on her bridal outfit, let alone, affect any last-minute alterations, which may be necessary. Slightly mystified, Margaret wondered who it might be. However, as after three seconds of de-fragmentation as the auto door of the 2P slid quietly opened, her question was soon answered, standing there gripping a small pink card for moment, a rather dejected looking Tim stepped into the room. The small, pink plastic card thrown hard against the far wall, fluttered aimlessly down onto the floor like a wounded butterfly and a day that had started out with so much promise, a wedding, a new son-in-law, a new Ford AVG and an upgrade in finance was now shattered…he had been retrenched!

"'I would not have minded if I was replaced by someone else,' he shouted, 'but another bloody robot, that's what hurts.' 'Today's stand downs, takes the human workforce redundancy tally to 85%.'

"'We can kiss the new transporter goodbye and at my age, God knows, if I will ever get another job,'" he said angrily while at the same time punching one of the grinning selection buttons on the refreshment consol. Then bending down, he picked up the cool tube of Dr Foster's medicinal barley brew (beer), which had rattled down the discharge chute and popped invitingly out of the slot at the base of the cabinet.

"Then for the first time in many years, he activated the controls on the sealed backdoor, leading to what had once been his garden-cum-barbecue area. As it slid quietly open, he slouched out into the steadily falling rain and headed towards the only refuge he knew, his large shed, filled with that old, sentimental junk.

"However, before the door could slide fully closed, Margaret called out to him. 'Don't go outside yet, Tim,' she said while glancing towards the 2P, 'Deidre is being projected.'

"As he stepped back into the cool air-conditioned room, the beeping sound from the 2P ceased as *'Bumph'*, the heavy, glass exit door slid rapidly closed to lock behind his back. One second, two seconds and then suddenly there was an almighty bang, followed by instant darkness. The doors which had slid closed behind him automatically locked as every light in the house exploded, and every electrical appliance instantly died a natural death, and worst of all, the 2P dropped offline with Deidre trapped somewhere in limbo… There would be no wedding today!"

Chapter 3
The Shed

"Tim had no idea what had happened, he simply assumed that due to an overload, a domestic circuit breaker had tripped out and the only way to find out if that was so, was to check it. However, as the sealed power distribution receiver and domestic circuit breaker systems was somewhere out on what was once the front veranda but now under a thick covering of ivy and inter-locking vines, which were now firmly attached to the front, if not all of the house; locating the cabinet would be a problem. He knew the box was on the veranda, but as it had been so long since anyone had seen it, just, where on the veranda, was a mystery. God only knows and he was certainly not about to tell anyone.

"'Hurry up and put the power back on,' Margaret called frantically. 'Deidre is in limbo somewhere, if we don't get her out of there she will fragment, and we will lose her.'"

"The first thing however was to get out and locate the power box, but as the electronic doors were now securely locked, manual efforts to open them failed. Taking a fire axe, Tim made his way through to the front of the house and attempted to cut a hole in the wall where he thought the back of the electronic distribution panel might be. Unfortunately, the modern, Poly-Carbon metallic impregnated fibre-moulded construction and UV insulation of the building simply absorbed the blows and the axe just bounced off the wall – he gave up in despair.

"'For God sake, call the electricians,'" Margaret begged, sub-consciously moving to the communication console where she feverishly pressed connection sequences. However, this once very modern state of the art, u-beaut communication system simply stared back at her with a blank glassy-eyed expression, it was dead …they were simply isolated.

"Today, for the second time in his life, Tim felt absolutely useless. Near panic and a feeling of utter despair, as he had never experienced before, engulfed him. It seemed that for the first time in his life everything was going wrong. He had lost his job, they had lost power, his wife was now hysterical, his only daughter was trapped somewhere in cyberspace and even the bloody cat was pregnant. In addition, to make matters worse, if that were humanly possible, during the power failure, he had dropped his cool tube of Dr Foster's medicinal barley brew. Now, in this electronically controlled environment, as frustrating as it was, he could do absolutely nothing to remedy the immediate situation…or could he?

"For many years, supported on its colourful brackets, in an ornamental glass case situated on the dining room wall, a large fire axe had sat smugly in all its glory. As the house was fire proof, it was as useful as tits on a bull, actually, it was more for show than anything else was, but rules are rules! Today however, after a lifetime of inactivity sponging on society, that axe was about to earn its keep. Using the other small axe, Tim smashed the glass and on removing the heavier axe, jammed the blade in the service panel on the side of the cool drink dispenser. On prizing it open, took out a cool tube of Dr Foster's. Then, sinking to the floor alongside the cabinet, he ripped the cap off and knocked back a few welcoming mouthfuls.

"'Is that all you can do?' Margaret screamed at him hysterically, 'sitting there on your arse, drinking bloody beer and our own daughter is trapped somewhere in cyberspace. If we don't activate that 2P she will disappear.'" At the same time after grabbing the can of beer out of his hand, she threw it against the far wall.

"Angry for the first time in his life, Tim shouted back in sheer frustration, 'I was thinking… God damn it.' 'You and your bloody Greenie mates are responsible for our daughter being in limbo, so don't bloody blame me!' he replied. "However, as she ran from one instrument to another in a state of sheer panic, checking them repeatedly for signs of life, she was not listening to him or anyone else… But sadly, everything electrical was dead.

"Tim, after giving it some thought, knew that the first thing he had to do was to get out of the house, he tried opening the rear door, but it too was now well and truly locked, he tried striking it with the back of the fire axe, which simply bounced of the heavy, laminated armour plate glass. While he stood there, desperately thinking of some way to break it, he once more scanned the room looking for anything that might suggest an avenue of escape. As he gazed around the room, coming into full view was the domestic safety box containing another fire blanket, a mid-range 6 Lbs-Co^2 fire extinguisher and a first-aid kit. Over the decades, just like the fire axe, the extinguisher, knowing that it would never be used, sat contentedly in its warm, little case.

"Breaking the glass, Tim took the extinguisher down and as he rolled it over in his hands, he now had bad news for it; its bloody freeloading days were over. Standing in front of the rear door, he pulled the safety pin out of the carrying handle and squeezing the trigger, discharging the entire contents onto the middle of the glass door over several minutes. As he concentrated the cold Co_2 vapour on one spot, the glass slowly began to chill, frosting up and turned white. As it contracted and shrank under the tremendous chill, the toughened glass creaked and groaned audibly. Once empty, he dropped the container, covered his face with one hand and hit the centre of the door as hard as he could with the back of the fire axe and, to his relief, it exploded into a thousand pieces.

"With the exception of a few moments ago, for the first time in many years, the warm, musty air bringing with it the stench of a decaying, dying city and rotting vegetation, rushed into the house; filling the long, empty sterile void of the large dwelling with a new aroma. Apart from electro projection, or in the sealed AVG, Tim had never physically been outside in years, well except for a few seconds a moment ago. Therefore, he had no waterproof clothing and as he dashed for the protection of the shed, he quickly became soaking wet.

"The large storage shed was not as well-equipped electronically as the main house, so it was not electronically locked or secured. So, opening the unlocked door, he entered and looked about. Without power there was no way of lighting the interior or seeing anything, so once unlocked and, with a great deal of difficulty, he pushed the large double doors that had once led onto the driveway, wide open.

The interior of the shed now flooded with a pale, misty light, illuminated row upon row of historical vehicles and equipment, and although he knew and loved every piece of equipment that was in here, he now wondered why the hell he had instinctively rushed out here. Slowly and as though in a dream, he walked along the lines of old assorted, antiquated vehicles and equipment until he came upon a four-cylinder diesel powered 50 KVA-240/415-volt AC/DC Duetz generator and there he stopped. This was just what he needed! Something, which could be used to energise the 2P for one second and get his daughter out of limbo. However, for fear of prosecution, as it had been so long since it had been started, would it work now that he so desperately needed it?

"This generator was a mobile unit, mounted on pneumatic tyres, tyres that were now of course virtually flat. So, dropping the safety fence around the exhibits, he managed by twisting it from side to side to pull it slowly but surely along the timbered floor up to the door. There in the subdued misty light, he set about starting it and being a qualified mechanical engineer, this posed no real problem.

"The first thing that needed to be done was to replace the stale diesel fuel, refill the tank with clean diesel and bleed the system through. Without giving a thought to the hefty fines, imprisonment or the bloody environment, he searched along the right-hand wall of the shed, which housed a complete tool rack. He found a set of metric spanners and with one, removed the drain plug situated in the base of the fuel tank and let the stale fuel go. As it gurgled merrily down towards the floor, he turned and hurried to the rear wall of the display shed, while behind him the old, stale fuel oil now having reached the floor, ran happily out the door into the rain-sodden earth.

Once at the rear of the shed, he ripped the environmental seals from the fuel pump system and using the mechanical hand pump, pumped up several gallons of clean diesel fuel from his secret cache. Then, returning to the generator to find the fuel tank, now empty, he replaced the drain plug and with the aid of a filter funnel, refilled the fuel tank. Discarding the engine cowling, he disconnected the injector feed pipes at the fuel injectors and placing a crank handle in the front of the engines harmonic balancer, after depressing the valve lifter; he cranked the engine over slowly several times. The purpose of which was twofold, (1) to bleed the clean fuel through to the injectors and (2), once the air in the pipes had cleared to make sure the engine would not seize to get up oil pressure. Once clean fuel came through, he refitted and tightened the injector pipes… In theory, it was now ready to start!

"Hidden away all these years in one of the many display cupboards, was a pressure pack of volatile aerostart or ether, had sat patiently waiting for just an occasion. Replacing the crank handle in the front of the engine, Tim lifted the decompression lever once more and slowly turned the engine over, listening intently for the tell-tale squeaking of each injector as it cracked under pressure. The squeaking noise of the fuel cracking under an injection pressure of 2000 atmospheres in the otherwise complete stillness of the shed, from an engine dormant for so many years; was like music to his ears. The injectors were not frozen or seized and with a bit of luck, the engine should start.

Picking up the can of aerostart, he shook it furiously and increasing the spin of the engine, he cranked it faster and faster, then spraying the ether into the air intake he let go the crank handle, dropped the decompression lever and for the first time in many years the engine fired. *"Ponk, ponk, ponk, ponk"*, it bellowed a few times before stopping. However, the puffs of white smoke being emitted from the exhaust pipe told him that the engine was going to work. However, after so many years of in-activity, the piston rings were most probably frozen or ring bound and it would need to get up a bit of compression pressure before it would run properly. Repeatedly, he cranked the engine up to speed and dropped the de-compression lever only to be rewarded with a *"Ponk, ponk, ponk";* the engine was certainly down on compression, the bloody thing just would not pick up and run properly.

"Not used to all this physical exertion in such a long time, he was now perspiring freely and in fact, had developed schoolboy's breaths, in other words his breath was coming in short pants so he momentarily leant against the wall to recover his breath. Then, between the laboured gasps of the warm humid air, it suddenly dawned on him how to get the engine going.

Years ago, when automobiles ran up and down the many highways that once cris-crossed the country from one state to another, one of his father's XJ6, 2.8 litre Jaguars was left for several days at 'Tullamarine Airport' car park in the city of Melbourne, Victoria. When required late at night, in the cold, damp wee hours for the return journey to Geelong, it simply refused to start. After several attempts to get it going, he called in the Royal Auto Club of Victoria who did not have a clue on how to start it. Finally, it was only after taking out the wet, fouled spark plugs and pouring a small quantity of clean engine oil down each spark plug hole into each cylinder to get additional compression, replacing the spark plugs with a clean dry set that the engine was made to work. Though he would admit, it was some time before the exhaust smoke from the burning oil coming out of the twin exhaust pipes at the rear of the Jaguar, cleared enough for his father to see where he was driving. Therefore, Tim thought if it worked for Dad all those years ago, then it should work for me now.

"Removing the injector pipes once more, he removed the two nuts and the flat retaining plate holding each of the four injectors in place and after removing them, tipped a measured quantity of engine oil down into each cylinder. He then cranked the engine over, slowly, to coat the cylinder liners and the piston rings with oil. Finally, after replacing and clamping the injectors into position, he re-bled the system and re-tightened the fuel pressure lines.

With everything ready, once more, he swung the engine over, faster and faster, then once more a short spray with the aerostart and on dropping the decompression lever, away it went.

"*Ponk, ponk, ponk, bang, ponk...ponk, bang, bang...ponk, bang, ponk, ponk, ponk*" and the engine commenced to fire on all four cylinders, running quickly up to full revs before settling back down to run smoothly on the governor.

"The smell of the diesel fumes and the mass exodus of many disillusioned spiders of all shapes and sizes and the odd smouldering cockroach quickly emerging from the, now rapidly heating, exhaust system, was really something to behold. After all the past dormant years, as the blue-white exhaust smoke of the long silent engine started to fill the shed; to an engineer like Tim, what a wonderful sound and smell it was. Cracking each of the injector lines again one at a time to bleed out the last remaining particles of air, as the engine roared along smoothly, he stood back and admired his handy work.

The problem now was to get the 240-Volt AC current being generated to the 2P before it was too late. So, grabbing his tool kit, he ran back inside and using the fire axe, he smashed away a false panel that housed the input wiring on the side of the control board and removed the input power plug to the 2P console. While the plug may have been a very fancy looking 4-pin variation of many other power plugs he had seen in his time, it was still three phases and still a four wire-four pin system. He could rewire the four-wire system from the Duetz to the console by simply chopping the wire off a short distance from the plug at varying lengths, then attaching it to the output lead from the generator console.

"More precious minutes ticked quickly by as he returned to the shed where using the blade of the fire axe, he frantically cut the lead off the generator plug and head down against the swirling rain, pulled the extension lead up to the house. With precious little time to spare, he chopped off the wire attached to the 2P plug, which was inserted in the console and coupled it to the four, bare wires protruding from the lead of the generator. Finally, with all the joined leads taped up and insulated from one another, he plugged it back into the console. As the settings on the 2P had not been altered, it should still work thereby completing the last programmed setting.

"Back in the shed and now armed with a piece of fine emery cloth, he cleaned the rotating slip rings on the alternator as they spun rapidly before him. Then leaning on the pick-up brushes with a piece of wood, he bedded them onto the clean slip rings and watched with delight as the cycle meter needle on the control panel rose slowly upwards, 20, 25, 30, 35, 40, finally to sit steadily on 50 cycles, spot on!

"Finally, he manually wound the voltage meter up slowly to 240 volts AC and with the cycle needle still steady on 50 cycles, he closed the circuit breaker. Inside the house as the energised 2P loaded up and completed its cycle, in the shed the valiant, little engine almost suffered a mechanical hernia as it leant over on its side straining to hold the sudden load. Now safely home, blissfully unaware that all that so-called, useless, rotten, old bloody rubbish in the shed had just saved her life, Deidre stepped from the 2P into the room. Late, a bit dazed, confused but very much alive. Margaret now crying tears of joy ran to the back door, called out, "'She is here, she is safe.'"

"With a sigh of relief, Tim dropped the circuit breaker out and let the engine idle down for a while to allow it to cool and normalise, before finally shutting it down."

Chapter 4
Not Only the Loss of Power

"On that fateful day, quite un-be-known to Tim and his family, two thousand miles or more away in central Australia, the rising water levels defying all attempts to keep it out had eventually flooded the national power generation and distribution system, which over a very short period had exploded. Scientist at work, employees and their families, along with townsfolk, who supported this unique township, disappeared in a violent, fiery atomic flash. The effects of this explosion and collapse of the generating system was felt not only in Australia, but also around the entire world. A world, which shared and relied heavily on the 50% power output generated and supplied by the national Australian power grid, which was fed into a global power system to support the world's high demand for electricity was in trouble… The only world that civilisation knew had now changed instantly.

There was no slow transmission to a new way of life, no warning, no preparation and definitely no training schools on how to look after yourself in the advent of a power failure. As pantries did not exist in the modern-day homes, there were no domestic stockpiles of food, no cooking equipment, and in fact anything to cook it on, nothing. The world's population was suddenly divorced from everything that had once supported it. From the richest in their ivory towers, to the poorest residents in their suburban cottages, no one was spared; they were all in the same boat...although strange as it may seem, thanks to the environmentalist of this modern day and age, no such contrivance or craft existed.

"On a day, which was supposed to be his wedding day, Wayne a communications officer and the intended bridegroom was at his place of work, out on the state-run fish farm, checking communication problems, which were being experienced. This very large piscatorial farm occupied the entire area of Corio and Stingaree Bay. It was a naturally enclosed area of semi-trapped tidal waters, a vast complex, covering some 3,000 square miles, situated on the shores of the City of Geelong at the very foot of Port Philip Bay in the state of Victoria.

The waters of Corio Bay were closed off to Port Philip Bay by a broad, natural sand bar, which crossed the bay from Avalon Beach to the north and Point Henry to the south. As surface shipping or international maritime cargo vessels were banned and never entered the once busy port. A sturdy wire-mesh fence had long since closed the entrance to Corio Bay from the main channel, which had been dredged through the sand bar, centuries ago. This channel allowed normal tides to flood the area with additional natural food and with the outgoing tide, clean the pens. It was an ideal location for such a project, a project that had not only been introduced by, but had spanned many decades of successful commercial fish farming in Geelong.

"The vast area of the bay was divided into many hundreds of free-floating enclosures or pens. The larger, deep-water fish and sharks being confined to the deeper sections, various mid-water species in the shallower parts and the smaller, sweeter species like whiting, mullet, bay trout, flounder and garfish along the foreshore shallows and sand bars.

"To service the fish farm, special anti-gravity work platforms were employed; these simply hovered above the placid waters of the bay and never disturbed the breeding pens or when feeding schools of fish. The platforms were not only designed to feed the fish and carry out maintenance within the farm, but were also adapted to net and remove selected species or pens on demand for the local and interstate markets on a daily or regular basis.

"Today, Wayne was trying sort out some communication problems, which were being experienced on the platforms, especially when working over certain species of fish. For Wayne, it was a day that had started out no different to any other and certainly gave no indication of the tragedy that was about to unfold. The suspect A/G platforms were checked in the main workshops with no apparent communication or control problems being experienced. As a last resort, it was decided to dispatch them out over the fish pens on normal feeding duties to see if the problems occurred over certain species when on-board electronic equipment was being employed.

"Check after check was carried out over the pens close in to the control centre, as well as those vehicles working a fair distance away on the extreme limits of the farm, with no apparent faults in transmission or controls being encountered. Then suddenly as one platform passed over the pens containing schools of yellowfin and bluefin Tuna, now close to the surface in a feeding frenzy, the transmission suddenly broke up. It was as though the communications to the work platforms were being over-ridden by a signal of similar strength and wavelength given off by the fish.

"'Mobile platform 17 this is communication's centre,' Wayne transmitted. 'I'm going down to 3.547 Megahertz, drop down to that frequency and give me a tuning call.'

"'Comm-centre,' the AVG operator signalled, 'this isssssssssss –' Then, as total silence followed an instant power failure – nothing.

"Within the communication's complex online computers, oscilloscopes (crows) and cathode ray test tubes along with the transistorised power cells that supported the complex, collapsed and exploded around him as they did instant darkness settled over the working area. Picking himself up and dusting the fragments of broken glass and pieces of burning equipment from his tunic, he looked out through the wide-glassed observation panels of the control-centre and could only stare in horror and disbelief at the spectacle unfolding before of him.

"The heavy and now totally disabled anti-gravitational platforms were all spinning out of control, crashing down into the broad fish pens and throwing the crews into the water. As it was now feeding time, the larger fish and sharks simply took to their change of diet with great delight. As all surface transport or watercraft were banned, these special A/G platforms were not designed to float and as they quickly sank out of sight, Wayne could only watch in horror as his work mates now struggling to get out of the pens, disappeared beneath the frenzied foaming surface. With no catwalks or other such platforms out there for them to haul out onto, attacked by literally millions of feeding fish, the occupants of the anti-gravity vehicles quickly disappeared below the once calm, but now blood-stained waters of Corio Bay.

Looking east towards the distant outline of the City of Melbourne, which is situated on the far side of Port Philip Bay, he watched in disbelief as large international cargo and passenger-carrying craft came crashing down into the choppy waters of Port Phillip Bay. Where for a little while, they wallowed like so many wounded whales before the cold seawater entered their red-hot Ion drive systems, causing them to not only explode but also erupt in great balls of fire and smoke, scattering debris everywhere. One moment they were there, the next instant they were gone, sinking quickly into the shallow waters of Port Phillip Bay with only their antennas protruding above the choppy waters to mark their final resting place.

Due to the power failure, the pandemonium and confusion out on the fish farm, Wayne was so busy putting out the fires, which had occurred because of the power failure that he did not notice the time, in fact it was about the time he should have been getting married. With the fires finally out, as there was nothing anyone could do out here anymore, his work mates were all dead and as there would never be any work out here again…well not in his lifetime, he felt he might as well head for home.

Ashore somewhere in a city now hidden beneath a vast native forest, as the inhabitants tried to come to terms with what had just happened, Wayne's thoughts strayed to home and his future bride. A bride he thought that was waiting patiently for him too materialises from the 2P. However, as he tried to repair his burnt and damaged UV work suit, little did he know that at that very moment, Deirdre herself was trapped somewhere in transit cyberspace.

"Until now, Wayne would have simply stepped into a 2P and projected himself to where ever he wished to go. Now, as the 2P did not work and there were no electronic or gravitational means of getting home or to Deidre's place, now without any known transportation aids, he would have to find his own way. However, as he had never driven or walked home, he was unsure where his home or in fact, where anyone's home was.

"Luckily, for him, the control centre on the fish farm was linked to the western foreshore by a permanent narrow walkway. This catwalk, used by VIPs or senior members for manual inspections of the shoreline pens, was situated high above the pens. Alternatively, in the old days it was used to deliver particular stores to the central control system and vehicle ramps. As the admin complex and workshops were a fair distant from the shoreline, Wayne, now surrounded by the pall of smoke billowing from the control centre and drifting towards the shore, doggedly made for the safety of the distant foreshore.

"Eventually, reaching the foreshore, he stepped down onto the sandy beach littered with shell grit. As this was the first time in his life that he had ever stood on the foreshore, or in fact any soil or sand, the sensation of it crunching away under his feet was hard to comprehend, but found it an incredible feeling. The unfamiliar sounds of his own footsteps crunching underfoot and the whistle of the morning wind as the tide turned and had commenced its run towards the heads was something he had never really experienced in his sealed controlled environment, or had ever taken any notice of before, and yet he liked it.

"As he stood there, getting his breath and trying to come to terms with his situation…undecided as to which way to go… or what the hell to do. Exiting the forest close to the foreshore, an elderly beachcomber crept silently up behind him and tapped him on the shoulder, frightened the living bloody daylights out of him.

"'Who are you? Eh…eh…eh?' the old man demanded aggressively, as he danced around and around him like a leprechaun wearing very tight underpants.

"'And what right do you have to stand on my beach,' he continued, 'I have been maintaining this area for 5 decades or more and all of a sudden you step onto it and start walking all over it as though it is yours!'

"'The power has gone off,' Wayne said holding his hand over his heart, trying to get over the shock of this strange greeting. While at the same time, gesturing with the other hand at the many specialised AG aerial equipment still spiralling down from outer space and plunging into the sea like so many hungry goony birds or pelicans in a feeding frenzy.

"'And bloody good enough too,' the old man shouted defiantly.

"'Just look at what those bloody idiots have done to my town,' he said pointing towards the large, green dome of the rain forest, a dome, which now covered, a once beautiful and prosperous city.

"'I'm sorry,' Wayne said defensively, 'but I never knew it as a city like you did, I was only born 2·35 decades ago, in fact, I have no idea where I live even.'

"'You wouldn't happen to know where Projection 36-28-3/052 is would you?' he asked raising a somewhat singed eyebrow.

"'I've haven't got the slightest idea of what the hell you are on about, projection what?' The old man replied still walking around him, apparently intrigued with his strange garb. Then as though feeling sorry for this mere youth, he asked, 'Did your parents ever show you any pictures of their home or their parent's home or ever mention where it was?'
"'Yes they did once, but that was long ago and I wouldn't recognise it now. I think I know more about my fiancée's home than mine,' Wayne replied.

"'Well…where the hell does she live?' the old man asked impatiently.

"Again, Wayne shook his head sadly; he had no flamin' idea and said so.

"'Well,' the old codger said. 'I have some historical material that might give us some idea as to where you or she lives, follow me.' And turning abruptly, he strode off south east along the sandy foreshore.

"Along the eastern beachfront, they walked past the remains of the once popular carrousel on the boardwalk in 'Transvaal Square', past the remains of the Royal Geelong Yacht Club with its marina still lined with row upon row of once proud yachts still patiently waiting for their crews… Crews that would never come aboard. Further along, they came to the 'Eastern Beach Swimming Pool'. Here in, days gone by this large salt-water bathing area was during the summer months, meeting place of the younger generation. Now, the once bustling kiosk, and recently removed from the eastern gardens, the four elegant cranes made of beaten copper sheet, symbolising peace and tranquillity, now over grown and decayed, stood on the edge of the children's wading pool.

"Without looking back to see if Wayne was keeping up, the sprightly old man passed around a narrow promontory once known as 'Lime Burners Point boat ramp' on the southern end of the eastern beach, again; long since disused and now choked with kelp and covered with seaweed. Then, turning southwest out of Corio bay, the pair came out onto the western foreshore of Stingaree Bay under what used to be the 12-gauge clay pigeon and skeet gun club range. Continuing south for a short distance, they came upon a foliage-covered yet elaborately tiled entrance to what was once a Lime Burner's cave, situated beneath a low cliff face, just a short distance northeast to the entrance to the fish farm. These caves were used in the late 18th–early 19th century to mine and burn lime for use in the manufacture of cement. Here the old man stopped and entered via a cloth-covered doorway. Inside the tunnel, which was dimly lit by several crude skylights, the old man by using the crudest materials had divided the area into several rooms. Wayne suspected that the depth, the tunnel was situated below ground, was probably the reason that the UV rays did not adversely affect the old man.

"The small area, in which the old man lived, was a treasure trove of antiquity, of books and domestic appliances. Of cooking utensils and assorted house hold items; of gramophones with assorted 33&1/3[rd,] plus 45&78 rpm records. It sported a treadle type Singer sewing machine. Old newspapers and magazines. Swords and guns. From corner-to-corner, floor-to-ceiling, wall-to-wall, history literally filled every spare, nook and cranny.

"Wayne was absolutely amazed; never in all his short 20·35 years, had he seen such things. He looked and touched as though he could not believe that all of this was real.

"'You mean to tell me that people actually lived with and used all these sorts of things in their everyday life?' he asked.

"'Too flamin' right they did,' the old man retorted with a touch of pride. 'No decent housewife would be seen dead without most of these things.'

"'Why in my day the women cooked and sewed, they knitted and made clothing for their children, went swimming, walking, out for bicycle rides and picnics, yep, they were certainly good times.'

"'Swimming?' Wayne queried.

"'Yes, swimming, that was where you get your gear off and dive into the sea or swim out into the surf to body board back to shore; or paddled your surf ski out to sea and ride the waves back to shore, that's if a white pointer (Shark) didn't get you. Sometimes just a quiet swim and a lie on the beach, sunbaking with your girl.'

"'You're forbidden to enter the water for pollution reasons and besides, I have never seen anyone laying on the foreshore sunbaking, not only is it forbidden, the Ultra-Violet rays would give you cancer,' Wayne countered.

"'Ultra-Violet rays, pollution, skin cancer, my arse,' the beachcomber retorted indignantly. 'I don't wear any silly bloody clothing like you and I am going on 9 decades old. I smoke occasionally; I drink plenty of home-made beer; I swim, I walk for miles along the foreshore, and I am certainly not burnt to a frazzle or dying of skin cancer.'

"'Your bloody boffins and so-called greenies have set you all up in such a fool's paradise that because of electronic transportation aids, you can barely walk and judging by the way the fish just ate all your mates, you certainly cannot swim either.' 'And I suppose,' he added, 'you have never had a beer or a smoke, and you are going to tell me that you have never had a naughty either.'

"'Naughty? No! My memory bank doesn't compute that, what do you mean naughty?' Wayne said with a puzzled look on his face.

"'It's an old-fashioned saying for having sexual intercourse or making love to your girlfriend, have you done that?'

"'As a matter of fact, no,' Wayne replied, 'one is never on one's own and you certainly could not do it while you are de-materialised in transit,' he continued, sounding somewhat indignant in the defence of his virginity.

"'And you call that bloody living,' the old man laughed while whacking himself on the thigh. 'Give me back my youth, a walk in the park and a cuddle with a pretty, young Sheila on the cool, damp grass any day.' He laughed and continued as though talking to himself, 'I remember an old saying, about some good-looking Sheila that after a night on the town went to sleep on the grass outside a synagogue and woke up with a heavy Jew on her.'

"'And?' enquired Wayne, somewhat puzzled by the seemingly innocent statement.

"'Never mind,' the old codger replied sounding somewhat exasperated. 'It has probably gone right over your head… Ah here they are!' he said, pulling out a sheath of musty, decaying maps of the city.

"'And what's all this?' Wayne asked looking at all the beautiful buildings, the tall steeple of 'Saint Mary of The

Angels Basilica' and the wide-open streets spread out over a vast area.

"'It's a map of Geelong,' the old man said proudly as a tear formed in his eye, welled up and trickled slowly down his leathery cheek.

"'Well, that's the way it used to look until the bloody greenies got in and you couldn't touch a living thing. Now of course, it is all over grown with weeds and foliage, it's still like that you know under all the growth and vines. One day, though not in my time, I'm afraid, it will rise up out of that man-made rainforest once more, now where were we?'

"'Oh, yes, where does that Sheila of yours live?' he mumbled.

"'I once heard Deidre's father say that they lived in a place call the West or something, so I probably could go there I suppose.' Wayne volunteered.

"'That would be right,' the old man said, his eyes lighting up as the memories of yester-year flooded back. 'That would be Geelong West,' he continued. 'That mob could even play pretty good football once; do you have any idea where in West Geelong?'

"'No, but Deidre's dad often used to joke about living in Royalty.'

"'Royalty, now you have got me there,' the old fellow mused. 'No, wait a minute, I might have it, did he refer to Elizabeth who was queen away back when?'

"'Yes I think he did,' Wayne said searching his memory. 'I know he had a medal for something from Elizabeth and they lived in a street of that name.'

"'That will be Elizabeth Street, I know where that is, and this man that had the medal for something or other, did he play football?'

"'Football, what the hell's that?' Wayne asked.

"Almost exasperated the old man put his hands to his face and shouted, 'It's a bloody game where you run around on the oval of a football field or the green grass of a park and kick a leather ball to one another.'

"'No, Wayne replied, 'you are not allowed on the grass, it is against the law.'

"'Oh, give me strength,' the beachcomber mumbled.

'Ah, there it is…that is Elizabeth Street,' he said stabbing a gnarled finger again and again at the map.

"'Come outside, and I will show you where it is,' and proceeded to usher Wayne unceremoniously outside.

"Using a set of stairs cut into the face of the cliff, which separated Limeburners Point from the former parkland above Stingaree bay, they climbed up the steep cliff face and over the top. Once on firm ground, the old man, pushing some branches out of the way, pointed away towards the northwest corner of the city, at the same time pointing out and naming the many prominent, tall landmarks, which were still visible even though well-covered with foliage.

"'There, that's where Elizabeth Street is, hang on a minute,' he said and disappeared back over the edge into his little dwelling, re-appearing some moments later with a small, brass military compass clasped firmly in his hand.

"'Here take this,' he said.

"'What the hell is this?' Wayne enquired as he stared at the strange, little brass instrument with its thin magnetic pointer fluctuating from left to right.

"'It's a blasted prismatic compass,' the old man shouted, any boy scout knows that, and don't you bloody dare ask me what a boy scout is!'

"Handing Wayne the compass, the old man instructed him to come and stand beside him. 'Just hold it steady until the needle settles down and it will be facing north.'

"'There…see!' he exclaimed with a twinkle in his eye, pointing to the needle, as it stayed steady on magnetic north.

"'Now turn the body of the compass around until the N for north is under the needle and that's magnetic north. Now, if you look at that large hump on the western horizon, which used to be the Geelong Cement Works at the top of Church Street, you will see that it is has a reading of 238 degrees west northwest okay? Therefore, what you need to do is to keep a few degrees to the north of that heading and it will take you to Elizabeth Street.'

"'So,' he continued, 'just head that way keeping the needle on north and that hump on 238 degrees start walking and good luck!' he called as he disappeared down over the edge of the cliff, and as suddenly as he had entered Wayne's life, he was gone.

"Now for the first time in his life, he was really alone and stories of the local dissident ferals flooded quickly into his mind filling him with fear. Mental pictures of these wild nomadic people that lived beyond and flouted the law, the barriers of the modern civilised society and the technological world, suddenly became all too real and so very frightening. From where he now stood, it seemed to him that just a tad more than good luck would be required to get him safely to Deirdre's place.

These so-called ferals, sometimes the hunted quarry in environmental, ethnic cleansing forages, lived out their lives as a rule, in total freedom beneath the vast forest canopy in a world of their own making. Planting their own crops, they lived off the land and the fruits of the sea, the latter readily available from the many pens in the protected fish farm in Corio Bay.

"Today, as Wayne headed in the direction of Deidre's home, battling through the tangled mass of undergrowth, vines and thorn covered clinging, wild rose bushes, thick scrub and heavy timber, for the first time in his sheltered pampered life; an unexplainable uneasiness crept over him, causing him to look constantly back over his shoulder. For the first time in his life, he began to experience the real meaning of fear. Were he and the old man all alone out here, or was the old man one of them too?"

Chapter 5
The Ability to Survive

"Over the years, for the sake of privacy, Tim had set up and run a communication network between family members. This secret communication system was one of the few nationally banned things that Margaret tolerated or simply turned a blind eye too. She felt that social security; SMS street cameras and being constantly monitored by Big Brother via a location-medical sensor and identification chip which is implanted in everyone's left buttock at birth, gave the local officialdom enough data on them without having their inner most thoughts and family conversations documented as well.

"Before the power failure, movement and travel was simple, for business purposes or during holiday periods, with the blink of an eye, you could be transported from one state to another. While shopping and movement around the local area via the 2P system was a normal everyday occurrence. Communications were instantly possible, simply by activating the visual-audio display system. This system enabled you speak via a translator and hear live, any language you wanted and to see whom you were conversing with the touch of a screen.

"Now, with the power and all known services such as food, water, sewerage and communications gone, the problem was how would the population, especially the younger generation survive. Today, most young mothers could do nothing in the home to feed and support their families. Even if they could, they had neither the equipment nor the basic food stocks in the pantry with which to do so. The once expensive robots and time saving devices were now useless metal cabinet; their once bright, shiny numbered eyes, now dimmed, stared vacantly at the far wall.

"Back at Tim's house, Margaret walked back and forth in frustration.

"'What are we going to do, Tim?' she asked.

"'Well,' Tim said hopefully, 'the first thing is to wait until the main news time, by that time the real situation should have been assessed. They should be able to supply enough emergency power from their storage condensers to transmit for a short period. Well at least long enough to let everyone know what the hell has happened out there and what to expect.'

"Meanwhile, out in the forest, a mile off so to the east, his clothing now torn and shredded, and his body bloodied by the tenacious, thorny clinging vines, blackberries, wild climbing roses and wait-a-while; Wayne stubbornly fought his way slowly west by northwest, staying as best as he could a little north of 238° true. Along many disused grass-covered streets he travelled, over the large, green humps and mounds that actually homes, concealed beneath the foliage, the panic-stricken residents now trapped inside. While here and there, passing many recently crashed and burning AGVs, but not daring to look in at the burnt, dying or dead occupants…there was nothing he could do for them, they were all beyond help. This tragedy for passengers and crew was in fact a windfall for the ferals who would quickly divest the dead and dying of their worldly goods and clothing.

"As Wayne got closer and closer to Deidre's home, the feeling that he was no longer alone became stronger, was he being watched? Followed? From time to time, he would stop and turning quickly to look behind, but whoever or whatever it was back there, simply melted out of sight into the dense foliage.

"As the vast overhead canopy increasingly obscured the last feeble rays of the late afternoon sun, darkness quickly began to close in about him. Then as he made his way around the base of a large, vine-shrouded tree, Wayne turned into what appeared to have once been a broad suburban street, or so it would seem. Lining both sides of the street, many large mounds were quite evident; these presumably were buildings or houses now covered with vegetation. As he stood there trying to come to terms with his situation, he found himself suddenly crushed to the ground by some thing or someone that had dropped down on him from high in the tree.

"The damp mouldy smell of rotting decaying clothing and stale body odour filled him with fear and desperation. Fighting desperately to stand up, he pushed this thing or whatever it was away from him. As this ragged spectre, that once was a normal human being fell backwards, struck its head with a dull metallic thud on a metal street sign pole long since covered by the sub-tropical growth slowly fell forwards to collapse at his feet. Now lying there quite vulnerable, male or female, he did not know he could not even hazard a guess. He could only stare at this ragged creature in disbelief.

Looking about to see if it was alone, he stared at the now exposed street sign.

"'Elizabeth Street,' the rusting street sign read.

"He had made it; Deidre's home was somewhere close by.

"As he stood there looking from left to right, a vaguely familiar odour teased his nostrils. He remembered smelling that odour a few times before, but what was it? Then slowly it dawned on him what that peculiar smell was; it was diesel exhaust fumes. He recalled smelling that same odour some years ago when for a few minutes Deidre's father had run up one of the engines in his shed.

"Following the breeze that carried the odour, after climbing up over and over several of the grass-covered dwellings, peering down into the tangled, matted backyards, he eventually came to Tim's house. After sliding down the roof and into the back yard, he staggered in through the smashed rear door and collapsed in a mongrel heap on the floor, right in front of his amazed fiancée.

"Tim and Margaret could only look on apprehensively as Deidre applied mouth-to-mouth resuscitation or so it appeared to the amazed parents. Then finally, the movement of arms that had suddenly enfolded their daughter's neck, seemed to indicate that the medication had done its job well and all too soon, as far as the children were concerned – it was time to prise them apart and find out what on earth had happened out there.

"'What happened out there Wayne?' Tim enquired urgently.

"'The power went off, that's all I know,' he replied.

"'It was terrible,' Wayne blubbered, 'the workers on shift out over the farm, all fell into the holding pens were all eaten.'

"'It was horrible, Mr Hawthorn. Those stupid bloody work platforms just fell into the breeding pens and sank within seconds, there was nothing I could do,' he said, covering his face with his hands as though trying to blot out the hellish image of his floundering, dying workmates being eaten alive by millions of feeding fish.

"Slowly taking his hands away and looking at the open door, 'I think you should barricade that door opening he suggested, I was followed here by some ferals, and one of them attacked me not far from here but was knocked out on the old street sign. Anyway…it was the smell of diesel fumes that got me here, so I guess it will not take them long to establish where we are by the smell of that exhaust smoke.'

"'True, very true,' Tim replied.

"'Look… I will look after the door while you see if you can rewire that 2P for a once only single projection transmission, I am going to try to get the family here. If things do come to the worst, which I believe they will, we will have a better chance of survival as a group,' Tim suggested as he headed for the shed to get a sheet of metal to close off the door area. With a temporary door now successfully bolted in place, Tim looked at his watch five minutes before 1900 hrs (7pm), just a few more moments until the emergency broadcast, that's if one would occur.

"'Do you think you could find us something to eat, Margaret… Deidre?' Tim asked looking towards his wife and daughter, 'I think we could all do with a cold tube and a bite to eat.'

"As both women left the room to see what they could salvage from the food dispenser, the entertainment console was turned on, they would soon know if it were possible to transmit and receive anything. 1859, 1900 hrs, slowly the large video screen began to brighten and the image of the new president of the republic, something that they just had to have, Paul somebody or other, stared blankly at the TV camera.

"'Residents of the Republic of Australia, it is my sad duty to inform you that the main power generation and distribution system at Fink in South Australia has been totally destroyed. Due to the constant rain, water managed to seep into the nuclear power generation system, causing it to explode and melt down. Sadly, all operators, families and other staff on duty in that region have been killed.'

"'This explosion has also created a radioactive no-man's land for a radius of 1000^2 miles, which I am informed by reliable sources, will remain radioactive for approximately 2000 years. Therefore, with no backup power systems, computers, or robots to build another atomic reactor or power system, we will have to start from scratch. This colossal venture, the manual designing and building of a new power system could take forty to fifty years, possibly into the year 2200.'

"'As you all know, due to past emission laws and regulations of the day, we no longer have any large steam, diesel powered or hydro-generation systems of the 19th and 20th century. Therefore, a panel will be formed to locate all former trades people made redundant by the recent switch to automation and robotics systems, which as you are aware are now useless. It will be your duty to design, assist and train the future trade's people of tomorrow to rebuild a power system for what we are sure can once more become a lucky country. While we can run this emergency EMF storage system, one transmission will occur each 7 days from now at this appointed time. To those of you who have lossssssst –' The transmission faded.

Lucky country my arse! Tim thought, visualising an old labour party cartoon he had once seen with a worker, a shovel, a camel and the following caption, which boldly stated.

"'Throw away your shovel, sit on your arse and light up a camel (cigarette), for this is the lucky country.'

"'Well, it was a lucky country before the present mob of bloody idiots got into power and now they want us, the people they could bloody do without, made redundant by robots and cast aside like rag dolls, to pull them out of the shit!'

"'No way,' he shouted angrily, 'no bloody way, that could take another century.'

"'How are you going with that re-programming, Wayne?' Tim asked looking towards the figure, hunched silently over a maze of wires and motherboards.

"'It's hard to say, Mr Hawthorn,' Wayne said looking up, I have no equipment or anything to test this type of unit, but if I am right, the single projection co-ordinate selection, which were programmed to this location when Deidre returned, should still work, the alternative is no one will be projected.'

"'I know that, Wayne,' Tim said, 'but what alternative do we have?' He knew that without transport of any kind, the rest of the family would never make it here. 'Close it up,' he called, 'and I will set up the ham-radio system.'

"Unbolting the steel sheet from the rear door, Tim made his way down to the shed. Where once safely inside with little trouble, he re-started the diesel generator and plugged in the 3-pin 240V lead from the radio transmitter to the control panel and turned the innocent looking radio transmitter, a radio that had been sitting there on the display shelf as an exhibit for years on and off. The re-assuring click coming from the radio speakers was music to the ears. This transmitter was fully functional and what better place to hide it than where everyone could see it.

Climbing up onto the roof of the shed, Tim cut away the ivy, clinging vines and creepers to clear the aerial hatch which allowed the 80-megahertz whip aerial, concealed inside one of the sheds tubular vertical support pillars, to be manually wound up through the roof into the air. With the hatch cleared from his vantage point up on the roof of the shed, he was able to look out over the city and the bay. Wayne had been right, scattered over a wide area, the smouldering wreckage of crashed AGVs were all too obvious. While there, he could also see people moving about down there. Who they were, he had no way of knowing, they could be residents who had broken out of their homes and now without power were simply lost and would soon become easy victims to the ferals. These ferals, hardened by their years of living off the land, would quickly take advantage of these physically and mentally weakened inhabitants.

"The 50 KVA generator was re-started much easier the second time. And once warmed up, Tim re-checked the lead to the radio and threw the switches on the radio to the 'On' position, watching with delight as the small output needle fluctuated from side to side each time he closed the transmit button on the mike, while tuning the set to its peak output.

"Setting the frequency for his number, three-son Dean, he commenced transmitting an automatic carrier signal, then sat back and thought about tomorrow.

"What was there for the family beyond tomorrow?

"What would he do if he did succeed in getting everyone here safely?

"Where would they go?

"If he did succeed in getting them all here, that would be only the start, he had to formulate a plan that would see his family and if possible, a few close friends and their children safely out of this area. Even this state or if they were to survive until the new era eventuated, out of the country altogether.

"'Indigo-Gamma-Hotel, this is Delta-Mother-Hotel, 1-2-3-4-5-6-7-8-9-10, do you read. Come in Indigo-Gamma-Hotel,' the radio crackled.

"Picking up the Microphone, Tim pressed the transmit button and called.

"'Dean, this is Dad, how do you read, over?'

"'Seeing that there is possibly no other transmission going on in Australia at this time, clear as a bell, Dad, what's happening? Over.'

"'The whole nation is now electronically and administratively dead, you and the family have got to get out of Sydney, is any of them with you?'

"'Strangely enough, yes, all the in-laws are here for Ryan's birthday, why? Over.'

"'Listen carefully, son, we are going to attempt to project you all here. I have started up the Duetz 50 KVA generator as a source of power and Wayne has rewired the 2P for a one-way transmission only. So, if you are all willing to take the only chance we have to get you all out of there, are you willing to take the gamble? Over.'

"Silence pervaded the warm humid display shed as nearly 750 miles away; a quickly convened round table conference made a once in a lifetime decision. The risk was high, however the alternative, unthinkable.

"'Indigo-Gamma-Hotel (Ivan Grosvenor Hawthorn), this is Delta-Mother-Hotel (Dean Michael Hawthorn) go ahead and set up the transmission, we are with you… I love you Dad…over.'

"'And I love you too, son,' Tim said, as he took a deep breath to choke back the tears which had suddenly formed and tried desperately to run down his cheeks…He could not go soft now, one way or another; he had to go through with it.

"'Okay, Wayne,' he shouted up to the house, they are going to give it a go, I will run the power lead up to the house as soon as I get them prepared, okay?'

"'Okay, Mr Hawthorn,' Wayne replied.

"'Indigo-Gamma-Hotel this is Delta-Mother-Hotel, it's all, go, Dad, set it up and we will get ready.'

"'Righto,' Tim said replied, 'now listen to me carefully, son, get Lisa to bring one only of her collection of antique cooking appliances, a coffee grinder, scales, utensils, anything that she feels will be useful to cook with.'

"'Get her dad to bring all the hand-held carpentry tools he can locate in the next few minutes and dress only in all your best cold-weather clothing and bring nothing else or we will over load the circuit.'

"'Once you have what you can bring, tape them or hang them under every one's clothing and cover them so they are part of the transmission.'

"'Oh, and by the way bring your samurai swords, we might need them, the natives are getting restless, if you know what I mean.'

"'Finally, when everyone is ready get them into the 2P and hold hands again to make it appear one object transmission. Once the signal is activated, insert our destination code and press transmit. When the transmit indicator comes up here,' he continued, while pointing unconsciously to a small dial as though Dean could see it, 'we will energise from here, God bless and good luck, son.'

"'Okay, Dad, see you soon,' and the transmission ceased.

"Tim switched off the radio and after disconnecting the three-pin power lead; he dragged the three-phase 240V, 4-pin lead up to the house once more and plugged it into the 2P. Wayne entered Dean's code as Tim returned to the shed to check the frequency and voltage now that the 2P was online. Everything set; he turned on the power and returned to the house to wait. Time slowly ticked by and with no air conditioning, the interior of the house aggravated by the constant warm, misty rain, the heat and the humidity was becoming intolerable.

"'What could be keeping them?' Margaret enquired with a worried expression on her face.

"'I don't know, but you know, Lisa! she's will hate to leave her antiques behind and probably bringing everything but the kitchen sink.'

"'I hope not,' Wayne cut in, if they overload the system they could cause the generator to drop offline and that would be the end of all of them.'

"'You have a point there, Wayne,' Tim said and suddenly volunteered, 'I'll go back to the shed and if the voltage begins to drop off, or if the governor fails to cope with the load, I'll bring up the revs manually.'

"Finally, the moment came, 'Mr Hawthorn, the transmit indicator light is on, they must be ready,' Wayne shouted above the roar of the generator, 'three seconds from now… go.'

"'One, two, three, energise.'

"'Once more, the gallant little Duetz generator belched forth…thick black smoke as it laboured to hold onto the load. The three-second cycle as it ticked slowly, seemed more like three hours, as Tim manually juggled the fuel throttle control to maintain the correct engine revs to maintain 50 cycles at 240V, for to over-generate would be as bad as a voltage drop. The easing off, of the load on the engine and the revs subsiding, indicated that the transfer had been successful. The other members of the family had been right, Lisa had brought enough antique equipment to start a shop, but the main thing was that he had proved that they could achieve a one-way transfer. All that remained now was to get the rest of the family here safely and this they set about doing. Finally, as the eldest son, Peter, his wife, Sharyn, their daughter, Lynda and husband, Matthew, both merchant navy officers were located along with their two daughters, arrived safely. As a decision on their future had to be made immediately, a round table conference was again convened and these were the points of reference.

"As it was obvious that it was unsafe for them to remain here, should they move and if so move where? Moreover, any decision they made…had to be unanimous. How would they move? What would they need to survive, in say, a totally isolated region? Would they take anyone from outside the family?"

Chapter 6
A Family Decision

"After due deliberation, it was agreed that they would leave Geelong, the consensus being that they would also leave the country of their birth and migrate south into the far reaches of the Southern Ocean. There, on an uninhabited island once controlled by the Australian Antarctic Division in the Shire of Esperance, then under the jurisdiction of the Tasmanian Government, they would establish a new community on that remote, deserted scientific station.

"This large uninhabited island laying at latitude 54°34' of south, 158 °30' of east in the South Pacific Ocean, once supported a large permanently manned weather, ozone study and scientific station staffed by twenty-seven to thirty people was Macquarie Island. However, with the passage of time and the introduction of automatic weather stations and solar powered satellite data transfer systems, as well as pressure from the environmental groups and green communities of the day, the station had been closed and left to the indigenous wildlife. The station, closed too and devoid of human inhabitants over several decades, the original inhabitants, the 'Children of Mother Nature', the penguins, elephant seals, the fur seals and the thirty-seven species of sea birds, indigenous to the region, had once more taken it back.

However, one thing was known and that was that the island was always fully stocked with standby and emergency stores. These mandatory stores accumulated over a period of many years by the members of ANARE (Australian National Antarctic Research Expeditions) wintering staff were in the event of AGV wreck victims reaching or becoming stranded on the island, retained and topped up annually. Best of all, none of these food supplies or equipment, had been removed. If supported by livestock and introduced reproductive foods such as, sheep, goats, red deer, poultry, and fish, along with local fish and krill from the surrounding seas, this vast storehouse of supplies should sustain them indefinitely.

"On arrival at their destination, they would introduce into the many secluded lakes, which abound the island, brown trout, large chinook trout and any other suitable freshwater species they might acquire from out on the state piscatorial farm, along with various crustaceans, which would be initially hand-fed before relocated into shallow lakes or tarns. This additional source of food would in fact sustain a small community indefinitely. It was decided that apart from the immediate family and friends, a group of ten young people of each sex or young married couples known to the family with children of compatible ages to their own would be invited to go. From this small group and their own children, the children beyond tomorrow, a future generation would be born.

"By radio, Tim formulated a plan with his number two son, Alan, his wife, Dorthe and their family, who lived down on the Bellarine Peninsular at Clifton Springs, where close by the small seaside community, still supported a long rickety wooden jetty, jutting out into Port Phillip Bay. Alan and his family would stay where they were until the great day came to move, when it did, they must be ready to commandeer by any means, at their disposal, a small herd of milking goats and two young Billys. In addition, a small flock of sheep and two young rams. Also, some red deer doe's and two bucks along with ducks, geese, and many fowls and a few roosters, as well as the feed for their menagerie, all of which was obtainable from the large nature reserve and wildlife park in Grubb Road, just a short distance from their home. Finally, cage the poultry for pickup and herd the livestock down to the jetty.

"At this time, as luck would have it, a flight of Senior Royal Australian Air Force Cadets under the watchful eye of the Sqd Padre was bivouacked on the spacious grounds of Alan's property. This flight was under the command of Alan's daughter, Emma, a cadet under-officer. Once the situation was made known to them and as it was obvious that they would never return home, this young group of well-trained cadets, both boys and girls quickly agreed to go. This now gave Alan, not only the man power at his disposal to complete his allotted task, a padre to act in religious matters and pastoral care and most importantly a group of teenagers, that would be the nucleus of a new generation beyond tomorrow.

"Among the many voluntary works he was once involved in. Tim was a committee member of the Melbourne Maritime Museums Historical Society and as such was aware that the 'Polly Woodside' a large iron barque, rigged three-masted sailing vessels. This Belfast built vessel of 678 tons, was built on the 7th of November in 1885. Designed as a deep-water vessel, she was 192.2 feet long with a width of 30.15 feet and a draught of 14 feet. This vessel had made many voyages around the world including several voyages around Cape Horn. Renamed the Rona in 1904 it was eventually sold to the maritime museum for one cent to be refurbished as a museum piece under its original name. With a compliment of no more than twenty including the captain and mate, she was the perfect vessel for their venture.

"Now on display and permanently docked in the Yarra River at the maritime museum in Docklands South Melbourne, it had recently been slipped and completely overhauled. During which time and much to the dismay of the nautical puritans, a powerful, 2000 Hp Caterpillar marine engine and two large fuel tanks had been fitted and filled with fuel to make it independent for use on festive days. Alternatively, the rare occasions when it was permitted out onto the river the vessel was kept completely fuelled, simply because of the emission and environmental regulation, there were no tugs on the harbour or the river to assist it any more. A b

A beautiful vessel which would follow the shoreline from Clifton Springs to the heads.

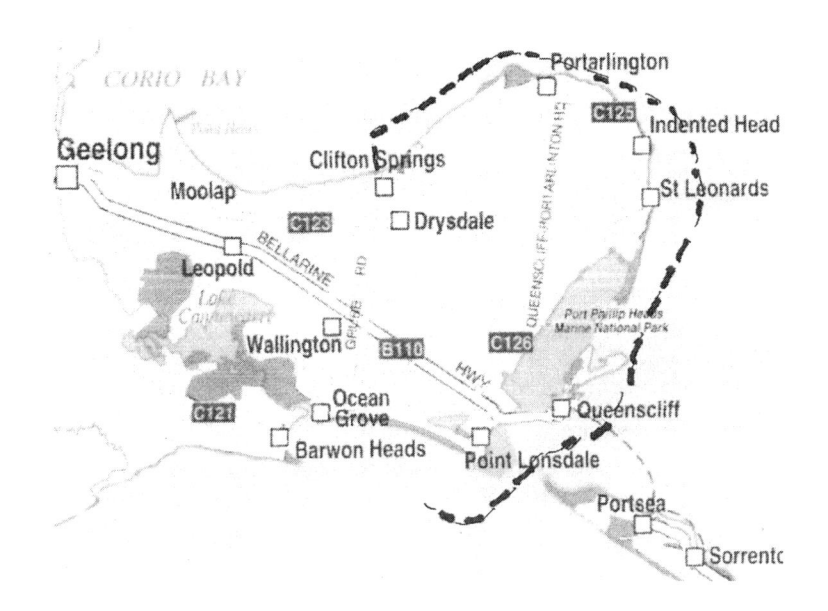

Travelling by sea and as their mode of transport, The Polly Woodside, which is self-supporting in every respect, was ideal for their enterprise thus giving them the best chance of reaching their destination. Again, to the dismay of the puritans, the vessel had recently been internally modified, and fitted out with four well-appointed cabins. These along with a small electrically equipped galley, which ran off the main generator/battery system was designed to cater for VIP dinner guests and civic functions.

"The rear poop deck area or approximately 50% of the rear deck area was surrounded or enclosed by a heavy weatherproof, re-enforced polythene curtain. This could be used as a shroud to close in the exposed forward deck area where the animals could exercise in good weather and to protect and house the larger stock, which for the duration of the voyage would have to remain exposed to the elements on the forward deck area. While the spacious cargo holds were ample for their proposed cargo.

"Now that the group had agreed on their destination, their mode of transport, all that remained was to get the vessel out of its permanently enclosed berth, turn it around, face it down river and get the hell out of there and onto the bay without being stopped, shot at or blown out of the water! On paper, it seemed a simple task, yet one fraught with danger. A great deal of thought was put into how best they could successfully achieve this, for now that they had committed themselves, there would be no turning back.

"Apart from acquiring the vessel, everything from toothpicks to tampons had to be obtained in the few short, frenetic hours, which would elapse between their departure for Melbourne, and the time the vessel arrived at Clifton Springs. This would include the acquisition of cold weather clothing and footwear. Many tons of assorted bulk foods, medicines, drugs and the latest medical operating equipment. Everything required to support this venture had to be obtained to a strict timetable, so by dawn when the newly acquired vessel would have presumably dock against the jetty at Clifton Springs, everyone and everything thing required to sustain them would be on the move or already at the jetty, ready to load.

"As no one had boats these days, or those who did had no fuel with, which to power them. Also, as marine craft had long since been forbidden on the water, no one really had any experience handling them anymore. Therefore, Tim felt that once they got the 'Polly Woodside' out of the river and into Port Phillip Bay, their task from that point on would be reasonably simple. To get the vessel out, they first had to remove the many barriers, which were known to be installed and cris-crossed the Yarra River at various intervals along its length up to the Docklands. Once they had achieved this, simply tow the 'Polly Woodside' out into Port Phillip Bay.

"At Tim's home, amongst the antique equipment and vehicles stored in the display shed, which he had so lovingly maintained all these years, were several large, heavy six-wheel drive military vehicles. Included in his vehicle collection was a large amphibious or light amphibious refurbishing craft (LARC), once used by the armed forces and in Antarctic refurbishing operations. Capable of carrying, plus fifteen to twenty people and/or 3.5 tons of cargo, this LARC was a very powerful, diesel-powered amphibious craft, capable of fast travel on both land and water. He also had an eight-wheeled drive Saracen armoured car, two x six-wheel drive GMC 10-ton capacity, stake side troop carriers and a few assorted APCs (armoured personnel carriers), and also two four-wheel drive personnel carriers completed the available vehicles.

"As the LARC was powerful enough to crash its way through the many barricades erected across the river, it was decided to re-enforce the bow with a sharp knife-edge aluminium blade and a team was immediately assigned to this task. Made of timber, the river barricades, which had been under water for many years, would now be very rotten and probably in the last stages of being decayed.

"Once they were in the river, armed with a mixture of homemade ammonia nitrate fuel oil explosives, they would blow the barricades on their way up to the Polly Woodside. Once their objective had been reached, someone would hop up onto the dock and once on-board the vessel, taking a towline, would run it back to the stern of the vessel, which was facing the river. Then once in position under the stern, the LARC would take the tow rope, on-board and pull the vessel out into the river. There, turn it around and once positioned under the bow, relocate the tow rope, now placed up forward and get the tow under way; eventually moving the vessel out into Port Phillip Bay while those on-board would steer her during the tow.

"Once the vessel was safely out in the bay, Tim along with his willing helpers would check and start the main engine. Having achieved that, taking the equipment acquired from the fish farm and those left in the LARC, on-board, would leave a set of explosives charges to blow it out of the water. The last thing they needed was to give anyone, anything that could be used to pursue and stop them in their quest to leave Australia.

"With the plan formulated, a few things needed doing before they lost the LARC. One was to find their way to the main dispensary at the local General Hospital namely Barwon Health and with someone with knowledge of what would be medically required for such a community to obtain what they needed.

"The second thing was to get Tim's father and mother, Ivan and Margaret out of the nearby retirement village. Ivan was not only a former automotive engineer but also a navigator of the old school. Better still, as he had twice wintered on Macquarie Island as the officer in charge of scientific expeditions, not only did he know where it was but he also knew what to expect from the local elements and how best to cope with them. Finally, Peter had to locate some ammonia nitrate prills, which once dampened with diesel fuel oil, would form his explosives; also, to set it off plain, No6 waterproof fuse and detonators. He would then make up 2lbs charges complete with detonator and fuse in cotton socks, which could be wrapped around the metal making up the barriers.

"However, as Tim could not take the risk of his plans being discovered by running around town in the LARC, it was necessary to change the plans and bring his other vehicles into play. Two of these vehicles would be the large, sturdy six-wheel drive World War 2 GMC troop carriers to pick up supplies. These vehicles were strong enough to push their way through the jungle and undergrowth that now covered everything in sight and carry the many tons of stores required.

"As he headed out to the shed to check out the vehicles and to get them started, he was confronted by several ferals dressed in rough, assorted garb and wielding spears and home-made halberd-like weapons, blocking his path.

"'Dean,' he called, backing slowly towards the house, 'we have visitors, and I think some of them are in the shed.'

"As if by magic, Dean the 10th Dan black belt Shogunate appeared in the centre of the backyard and stood leaning forward on his right leg forward with the knee slightly bent; a typical samurai stance and without turning his head seemed to know exactly where everyone was. Then as if tired, he deliberately crossed his legs and slowly sat down cross-legged with his arms extended along his thighs, palms of his hands facing upwards in a lotus position. Taking this as a sign of submission, the group of ferals leapt forward and stooped down to grab him.

"After laying idle in its scabbard for many decades, with the smoothness of a piece of silk, the long, thirsty virgin blade of the razor-sharp Katana suddenly appeared in his hands and on completing a 360-degree arc, the severed heads with their disbelieving eyes staring blankly at the falling rain, rolled crazily around on the damp earth. With a flick of the blade to remove the tell-tale signs of blood, it was wiped dry to disappear back into its scabbard, all in one motion. From inside the shed, the remaining ferals witnessing this terrible feat leapt empty-handed through the open doorway to disappear into the safety of surrounding canopy. Moving the stale headless bodies and heads out of sight into the nearby foliage, Dean, totally unaware of the steadily falling rain returned to his lotus position in the middle of the yard to meditate.

"Once more, back inside the shed, Tim organised a group to get the air compressor going and inflate the many semi-flat tyres on the selected vehicles, and to check the pressure of those still inflated. Taking a number of 12V batteries from the charging rack, after checking and topping up the acid levels and replacing the tops; he began fitting them to the various vehicles. Meanwhile, outside in the steady-pour rain, his meditation broken by the steady beat of the long stroke GMC petrol- and diesel-powered engines as they were started and warmed up to settled down to a steady beat. Dean stood up and moved into the shed. Inside, sparks flew wildly about the shed as the cutter plate for the bow of the LARC was fashioned and made ready to be bolted into place."

Chapter 7
The exodus

"With every family member accounted for, except for a few close friends who would be given the chance to join them once everything started to roll, it was time to get them on site. And these were Mitta (Adrian) Moody, a retired engineer, his wife, Sally and their family. Sally was a member of the local spinning guild, and could do wonders with raw wool or fibres, also spinning and dying wool, sheep, angora goat and natural fibres. In the coming years as their immediate wearing apparel began to deteriorate, these were skills that would be absolutely essential to the survival of the group. One of their children was a teacher and fortunately for us, she was married to a doctor, something we desperately needed. Again, education was something that the children of this proposed group and their children would need, the job of locating and projecting them on site was left to Wayne.

"Another friend, Mr MacFarlane, known affectionately as 'Barry Mac' was a qualified butcher and his expertise in this field would ensure that the livestock was dressed properly when it came time to slaughter them for food. His family, none of who possessed any real technical skill other than banking, would soon adapt. However, on second thoughts, one was married to a dentist so if they came, medically they were pretty well covered. Although, the house was now getting crowded, they had to get them all here as quick as possible, for as soon darkness settled in; all the raiding parties would depart to complete their objectives and any one not here, would be left behind.

"One by one, Wayne contacted those invited and for those coming, entered the projection code for those invited, and as a transmit light beamed on; on our console, he projected the amazed families into our house. Now that it was all go, there was no time to bring anything for they would simply join in the raiding parties that were going to hit the various supply stores, dispensaries and warehouses for the many hundreds of items the group would need to survive.

"Robbin the Doc, using a four-wheel drive Dodge Weapon carrier would follow an APC (armoured personnel carrier) that could push through anything, and would lead the raid on the hospital's pharmaceutical store. There he was well known and making out he was preparing to leave for 'Fink' with the medical supplies, in the dark and the confusion he would not be questioned as he acquired everything needed with little or no trouble.

"Mitta Moody, along with his family, and Wayne driving two of the large six-wheel drive troop carriers would hit the bulk food warehouse in East Geelong and acquire as many tons of bagged, self-rising flour, sugar, malt, and the many tons of assorted groceries, which would complement what we assumed to already be on Macquarie Island.

"Driving a multi eight-wheeled Saracen armoured personnel carrier, Barry Mac and family would, after picking up Tim's parents, 'Ivan and Margaret' from the old folks home and followed by the other troop carrier, would look after the cold weather clothing by raiding the ski and mountaineering suppliers in the city of Geelong. Waterproof quarpel jackets and pants, thermals, under garments for male and female alike. Woollen pants and mountaineering shirts, parkas; shawl, necked jumpers, wet-weather clothing, mountaineering boots and socks, beanies, gloves and balaclavas headed the main list of requirements.

"Meanwhile, Alan, his wife, Dorthe, their five daughters and son, Dominic, along with the twenty cadets would head for the animal sanctuary and fair ground in Grub Road. For if the raiding party to Melbourne was successful in securing the sailing vessel, by the time the Polly Woodside lay up against the ancient wooden jetty at Clifton Springs the following morning, everything they were expected to obtain had to be there waiting.

"After a final briefing, Tim, Dean the 8th black belt Samurai Shogun and Peter, a naval officer come explosive man, climbed on-board the now modified and reinforced LARC and after much pushing and shoving, they made their way up over the dense foliage covered front drive of the house and picked their way cautiously down to Corio Bay. Once safely in the water the drive wheels were disengaged, the steering locked dead ahead, the propeller drive and rudder engaged, they crashed their way through the dozens of flimsy floating fish pens out across Corio Bay to the deserted piscatorial control centre, where they came alongside and tied up.

"Climbing up into the now deserted office, hatchery and storehouse, where from the breeding laboratories they helped themselves to as many sealed plastic transportation containers of freshwater trout, redfin, perch, and bream fingerlings. Freshwater yellow belly and bass fingerlings as they could carry. Along with millions of fertile murray cod, perch and redfin eggs and fingerlings, also thousands of freshwater yabbies, shrimps and without dangerously over loading the vessel, all the large Tasmanian black freshwater crayfish and the palletised fish food, the LARC could safely carry.

"Once their booty was safely stored on the deck of the LARC, tied down and covered, they continued their way across Corio Bay, smashing through the many holding pens before finally engaging the drive assembly. Once more, crawled up over the broad sand bar separating Corio Bay from Port Phillip Bay and dropped down into the waters of Port Philip Bay; where they engaged the propeller drive once more. However, before heading for Melbourne, they took time out to motor up too and blow up the retaining wall across the main channel linking Corio Bay to Port Phillip Bay, thus allowing the millions of once-captive fish to depart for the ocean, an ocean they had never known. With that last act of open defiance, the die was cast and there was definitely no turning back now.

"As the piccaninny dusk settled down to the incredible darkness of night, the LARC roared on towards Melbourne. Along the way, passing many sunken or partly submerged cargo carriers and international passenger craft, with the bodies of their hapless crews and passengers trapped inside or floating face downward in the dark, choppy waters of the bay. As there was nothing anyone could do for them, they motored quickly by.

"From out here on the bay, the huge outline of the vast, darkened, foliage-shrouded City of Melbourne looked grim and un-inviting. No sign of life, nor the flicker of a light was visible; it was as though nothing or no one had ever lived here. All that could be distinguished was the outline of a vast, darkened Forest with the tops of the once-proud sky scrapers and church steeples breaking through the canopy like grotesque fingers reaching up towards the night sky crying out for help.

"Help…that would be a long time coming!

"Once in the Yarra River, as there was no shipping permitted any more, channel marker lights or navigation markers/buoys were not used. Now with the exception of a few solar charged battery-powered channel lights, navigation was going to be difficult. Without using their own lights, which would give away their position, it was not going to be all that easy to even find their way into the mouth of the Yarra River, let alone navigate an un-marked arm of the river. However, Tim felt that if he homed in on the tall chimneystacks of the old disused Yarraville Power Station on the port side of the entrance, and committed the LARC to the starboard side of the riverbank he should be on track. They only had one chance to succeed, for once inside the dock lands area; the fireworks would start.

"Meanwhile back in Geelong, with the departure of the LARC, the area around the house was alive with activity. As all the vehicles were re-started, the eternal silence of suburbia was suddenly shattered by the steady roar and revving of the various engines. The clashing and grinding of gears, as the unskilled drivers tried desperately to engage and disengage the long, frozen clutch plates to get the vehicles into gear and manoeuvre out of the shed, was ear shattering.

"As the clutches were being freed and vehicles moved out into the back yard, the future expeditioners moved quickly about loading what precious little there was to be taken from the house. Finally, with everyone on-board, hatches were closed; tarpaulins pulled tight and tied down securely to stop unwanted visitors getting on-board while in transit. Then without a solitary backward glance, one by one, the column roared up over the undergrowth and out onto what was once Elizabeth Street. There, following the tracked APC and the armoured car, the small convoy crashed its way along Elizabeth Street, down Church Street towards Packington Street and the city and the many other scheduled destinations.

"As the vast majority of the migrating families had never experienced the rocking, jolting sensation of being driven in an earth-bound vehicle, for most, it was an incredible, if not a darn right frightening experience. The feeling that they were about to roll over at any moment, or as the nose of the vehicle climbed high into the air as it negotiated dead or rotting trees, undergrowth and even small buildings tucked away out of sight, made them hang on for dear life.

"Passing a wide-open space that was once the Geelong Golf course on Thompson's Road in North Geelong, the armoured car braked suddenly and the head and shoulders of Barry Macfarlane appeared out of the gun turret hatch. Holding up his hand, he signalled the convoy to stop and wait here. As the forest and the undergrowth was so dense in this area, Barry felt the convoy would not reach the city limits un-aided.

"'Wait here while we get Ivan and Margaret,' he called, 'they are only half a mile from here, I have not spotted any feral movement but for safety sake, stay inside the vehicles, okay?' and dropped out of sight. With a loud roar, the armoured vehicle leapt forward and locking up the right-hand bank of wheels, pivoted around to the right and headed out along what was once the main highway leading to the City of Ballarat. As the heavy timbers had not yet penetrated the once sealed highway, he made good time to the main gates of 'Grace Mackellar' rest home where turning right once more, he drove up and over the gates and into the No.5 cottage area. Leaping out of the vehicle, our dentist, Ron, forced his way into several small, self-contained cottages and as luck would have it soon found Ivan and Margaret; somewhat bewildered but glad of the company.

"'What the hell is going on out there?'

"'What happened to the lights?'

"'Where are our meals?' they both asked without taking breath.

"'Sorry, Granddad and Grandma, I haven't got time to explain now,' Ron answered. 'Look, all I can say is Tim sent me to pick you up; we are getting you out of here,' he continued.

"'Thank God for that,' Ivan replied, hastening towards the bedroom door to get some personal things.

"'I'm sorry Granddad,' Ron shouted after him, 'there is no time to pack anything; all Tim wants you to bring is your collection of southern latitude nautical maps?'

"'But what will we do for clothing and other things,' Margaret asked sounding somewhat bemused and lost by the rapid course of events.

'I'm sorry, Nana , but we can't wait to pack anything,' Ron said urging her towards the door and the waiting vehicle. Ivan re-appeared from his study with a large roll of nautical maps tucked securely under his arm and followed them out into the steadily pouring rain.

"'That's one of my old vehicles you have got there,' he said with a degree of satisfaction, 'I knew they would come in handy someday.' Willing hands helped them both through the heavy rear bat-wing doors of the vehicle and no sooner had the steel doors clanged shut and the handles locked closed, that the vehicle surged forward.

"Meanwhile, back at the corner of Thompson Road and Ballarat Road, the rest of the convoy personnel were getting anxious as several ferals appeared out of the undergrowth to look in fright at the snarling, roaring collection of vehicles. Adrian, better known as Mitta Moody and the other drivers nursed the engine revs up and down as they tried desperately to keep the engines cool. Here due to the protracted idling period, the water temperature in the engines was rising steadily, but in case they never started, again…they dare not shut them down.

"The ever-inquisitive ferals, slowly overcoming their fear of these strange looking machines, became increasingly curious. Having never seen anything like this before, they did not really know what to make of them. Luckily, they did not realise that there were people inside them. If they did, the situation would soon change and most probably for the worst.

"Then, just as the entire feral's group started to emerge from the undergrowth and converge on the column for a closer inspection, the roar of the approaching armoured car could clearly be heard. Using the track it had cleared on the way out; it roared quickly into view and making a quick pass around the waiting column sent the terrified ferals fleeing for cover.

"Once more under way, the convoy made its way into the city and stopped at the mountaineering distributors. Here they reversed the heavily protected armoured car into the building, smashing through the front door and windows. While there was certainly no ammunition in the gun turret, the long, evil-looking barrel of the 50mm cannon traversing from left to right was enough to persuade the few workers trapped inside the building to leave hurriedly through the shattered window and flee out into the night. Removing the armoured car, they backed a troop carrier in through the damaged front of the building and into the display area. The large APC drove into the hole closing it off to outsiders and using its headlights, illuminate the dark interior.

"'Every one out, let's get everything we want,' Adrian called as he undone the rear tarpaulin, allowing the passengers to climb out of the vehicles and working with the aid of the headlights, they systematically acquired the many tonnes of cold weather clothing for both male and female members, young and old. Thermal underwear, foot ware and socks, headgear, pants, shirts, jumpers, mittens, snow glasses and gloves of every size, and so the list went on. The additional equipment taken from display cases, were several boxes of heavy fishing line, boxes of large hooks and sinkers, several long game fishing poles and associated fishing gear, such as spinners and lures for use during the voyage.

"Finding the vault which had remained wide open when the power failed, they acquired several cases of ·22 calibre rounds of extra-long .22 pea rifle ammunitions, amounting to many hundreds of thousands of rounds as well as several thousand rounds of assorted 12-gauge shot gun cartridges found stored there, this was equivalent to ten cases of each.

They also found several brand new yet historical weapons of the same calibre as the ammunition, which were housed as display pieces in sealed cases. These weapons would complement those known to be stored on the island for hunting rabbits and deer.

"'Don't take anything we don't require or we will run out of room,' Adrian urged, 'just the clothing and hunting equipment.'

"With the vehicle loaded to the hilt, they drove out onto the street and heading east along Eyrie Street, and soon came to Barwon Health General Hospital. Where they once more backed up against the loading ramp and using the long barrel of the 50-mm cannon as a very effective ram, forced the door in and backed one of the troop carriers up against the door. Led by Robbin the Doctor, who stated that they were here on an official mission of mercy to acquire medical equipment and supplies for any survivors, which might be found alive in the Fink River Power Station area in the State of South Australia. He enlisted the help of what staff they encountered and successfully acquired several tonnes of assorted medicines. Also, drugs, anti-biotics, toiletries, maternity equipment, anaesthetic and the latest modern portable computerised surgical operating equipment. With the help of the willing medical staff, they loaded their booty into the appropriate truck and once tarped down quickly, took their leave.

"The sun having long since set, darkness made navigation quite difficult, and several dead ends were encountered before they eventually arrived at the vast, deserted bulk food warehouse in South Geelong. The steel shutters, roller doors and electronic aids may have kept the Ferrell's out. Now, with the electronic surveillance off, it had no hope of keeping out a very aggressive 3.5-ton armoured car. After two or three hits with the rear of the vehicle, the steel shutters buckled and after forcing their way inside, as they were not just going on a picnic, took only what they required to last them until they were able to support the group with locally grown foods, meat and fish. Items such as flour, sugar, tea, coffee, yeast, jams, honey, vegemite, dehydrated and tinned vegetables, pickles, salt, pepper, and other assorted condiments. Hundreds of gallons of assorted pure essence, assorted dried fruits and a vast supply of various packets of vegetable seeds.

"Four-gallon containers of white and brown vinegar. Many four-gallon containers of spring water and cooking oil for the impending voyage. Many 50lbs. drums of malt and white sugar for the production of home-made beer, along with tons of assorted ten-gallon casks cartons of red and white wine, port and bottles of assorted spirits. Midnight came and went as almost twenty tonnes of assorted food had been loaded on aboard each of the 6-wheel drive troop carriers.

Two large twenty-seven foot tandem-wheeled trailers once used to move products within the bulk store were commandeered and twenty-two tons of assorted food, including several tons of dehydrated potatoes, onions and assorted vegetables were acquired. For the little ones, tons of assorted sweets and chocolates were loaded as well into the second weapon carrier. And finally, stacked where ever there was a bit of room left, on the roof, on the running boards, on top of the gun turret, hundreds of cases of Doctor Fosters medicinal barley Brew (beer) were the last item to come on-board, a lad has got to have a cool tube at the end of the day you know! Once everything was securely lashed down, the trailers coupled to the troop carriers and happy with the eighty to hundred odd tonnes of assorted food supplies they had acquired, they moved out into the night.

"Again, a broad six-lane highway that had once carried thousands of tourists and local residence around the beautiful Bellarine Peninsula was still serviceable, even if it was shoulder-high with grass and vines. Luckily, here again, no heavy timber or trees had penetrated the sealed surface; and while their progress was deliberately slow, it was possible. It was also worrying that the constant low gear operation and pulling such heavy loads, that the temperature of the engines was still rising dramatically; most of them near to boiling point. If they continued to overheat at the present rate, the engines would boil and the engines eventually seize, thus ending any chance of a long-term survival in a remote, geographically hostile area.

"At Grub Road, a major arterial road, which linked Drysdale/Clifton Springs with the Queens cliff Highway, the convoy turned left and pulled up. Here they cleared the mass of debris, grass, seeds and fluff from the radiators. It was this material which was blocking the radiator core, was obviously causing obstruction to the airflow over the cooling fins. Once cleared, the temperature gauges immediately commenced to drop towards normal and they were free to continue.

"Mobile once more, the heavily laden convoy pushed its way slowly down Grub Road towards Drysdale, a distance of some six miles, the last few to Clifton Springs and the foreshore of Port Philip Bay. As they made their way slowly along Grub Road, they came upon Alan, Dorthe, their family and the group of cadets now making their way towards the animal sanctuary. On coming to a halt, Barry called through the small opening in the door of the armoured car.

"'G/day mate, out for an early morning stroll,' he ventured.

"'G/day yerself,' Alan quipped.

"'No, as a matter of fact we are going to collect the eggs.'
"Pointing down the road to the wildlife sanctuary, they were approaching.

"I tell you what, Barry,' Alan said, 'get the other drivers to fan out a bit behind you from left to right and flatten the undergrowth, that will make a decent track for us to move the stock down, okay, see ya.

"'Come on you lot,' Alan called to his party and they quickly disappeared into the darkness.

"'Good luck,' Barry called as he opened the top hatch and climbed out into the night. Hurrying from one vehicle to another he conveyed Alan's suggestion and hurriedly returned to the warm humid, yet dry interior of the armoured car.

"At the same time as Alan and his group arrived at the wild life sanctuary, the convoy arrived at the edge of the sea. Making its way down the steep embankment to the foreshore and having backed the trailers up to the edge of the jetty, they used the heavily laden vehicles to flatten the undergrowth by driving back and forth, cleared an area where the stock could be held. Once the area was flattened, they backed the convoy of vehicles up alongside the trailers at the edge of the jetty, and immediately commenced to unload the cargo.

"Meanwhile back at the sanctuary, the vast array of penned animals were so used to visitors, being patting and handled, that they simply walked up to the poachers as they opened the various pens. Collecting as many transport cages as they could locate, the group assembled the required poultry and feed. With no surveillance equipment on and the game wardens now locked in their darkened quarters, their presence simply went unnoticed. As the first grey tinge of the piccaninny dawn lit the rain-shrouded sky, Alan and his merry band of rustlers, complete with their menagerie of assorted animals, and following the clearly marked trail left by the convoy, were well on their way to Port Philip Bay, the jetty and a new way of life.

"The first vehicle unloaded at the jetty was restarted, and immediately headed back to the wild life sanctuary to collect the caged poultry and several tons of feed for the stock."

Chapter 8
Not Your Usual River Traffic

"Far across Port Philip Bay, at 2300 hours or 11 PM, Tim had turned the LARC hard to port and lined up the mouth of the Yarra River, a river, which runs through the heart of the City of Melbourne. As he thought, a sturdy electrified barricade closed it off to water traffic. Further ahead and quite visible just above the surface the dark waters of the river many more barricades could be seen.

"'Oh well,' they had to start somewhere. At least the power to the barricades was off, so that was something. Idling up alongside the first and most impressive of these barricades, with the side curtain on the deck of the LARC removed, Peter lit the waterproof fuse on a plastic sock full of ANFO (Ammonia nitrate fuel oil) explosive and laying down flat on his stomach, leant down over the side of the vehicle. Extending his arm deep into the water and squeezed the sock over a beam beneath the water line and once happy with the position of it, stood up and called. 'Okay…let's get to hell out of here.'

"Selecting reverse gear, Tim backed away from the rising, smoking bubbles given off by the burning waterproof fuse and motored out, away from the mouth of the river. Going forward, to absorb a little time, he steered further to port and swung the craft around in a wide arc in the darkened estuary before straightening up and heading back towards the barricade at full throttle. As the vessel closed rapidly on the barricade, Peter kept counting down the burn time of the fuse and as they rapidly approached the smoking bubbles rising from the burning fuse, it appeared that they might have been a tad hasty. The closer they got, the more likely it now seemed that they were about to blow themselves out of the water: had Peter miscalculated the burn time of the fuse?

"As the vessel was almost upon the barricade, Tim, as he watched the bubbles still popping happily on the surface, had already gone hard astern, when the water around the barricade suddenly erupted violently into the air. Re-selecting forward drive and without as much as a bump they picked up speed and roared through the gaping hole in the barricade beneath a shower of falling debris and water.

"'Phew…was that ever close?'

"Again and again, they repeated this exercise until they finally came to the last barrier, which combined a narrow catwalk and led from a large exhibition building irreverently known as 'Jeff's shed', a former premier in years gone by to the Polly Woodside. In its little, sealed enclosure, this catwalk separated the 'Polly Woodside' from quietly moving muddy waters of the Old Yarra River. However, the echoing sounds of the rumbling explosions had drawn the flies, over the last few hundred yards; a few security police had appeared along the banks of the river and fired a several weakened laser bolts at the shadowy outline of the LARC. Luckily, the weakened, ill-directed laser bolts, which were being fired in all directions, luckily missed the small moving target.

"As the vessel approached the Polly Woodside, it was obvious by the number of people gathered on the stern section of the vessel that they also had a welcoming committee. Several ferals brandishing their crude weapons stood defiantly at the stern of the vessel hurling their weapons at the incoming LARC. However, sadly it was too late to worry about them now. Dean while standing over Peter, as he lay on the deck of the LARC planting the last of the explosives deep under the water, contemptuously flicked aside the incoming shower of spears and other projectiles with the blade of his katana. As they had no more need of any more explosives, several charges were planted down into the murky water on each side of the boom gates come – catwalk and in reverse once more, they idled slowly back out into the river, well out of range of both ferals and the coming explosion.

"'*Boooom, boooom*', for the last time, the dark muddy water of the river spewed skywards; carrying with it, planks, debris and pieces of metal hand railing and timber from the catwalk decking sailed skywards to splash down all around them. As it settled, they roared in towards the little dock and once up, against it, Peter and Dean jumped ashore and ran quickly along the dock and up the now heaving gangway onto the vessel. Meanwhile down on the turbulent, heaving water, Tim turned the LARC about and began reversing in under the stern of the vessel.

"On board, the unexpected welcoming committee was waiting for them. As the boys raced up the gangway, the group of Ferals re-appeared at the top, blocking their path, but having no time to stuff about the katana and the small but deadly Wakezaski gleamed in the diffused misty moonlight and the welcoming party lay scattered about the deck, no longer part of this world.

"Pulling the pins out of the gangplank pivot, they dragged it up and let it fall on the deck, then Dean, running the length of the vessel, with a single sweep of his samurai sword, cut through the thick, mooring ropes as he went. At the stern, Peter dropped a heavy mooring hawser down to Tim, who had now positioned himself under the stern of the vessel. Looping the hawser over the rear bollard, he made his way forward into the cabin and putting the craft into forward gear, increased the revs.

"With the last restraining hawser cut, the noise the movement of the large vessel, which was now underway, brought several immature Ferals up the companionway from the cabins. Shrieking and flaying the air with spears and all modes of antique weapons, they rushed towards the men at the helm. However, strange as it may seem, the sobering sight of their headless companions laying quietly on the deck and the deadly samurai swords gleaming in the misty light, without a spoken word, encouraged them to dive over the side and disappeared into safety of the cold, dark waters of the river.

"After centuries of being land locked, the great vessel seemed to know it was free for as they swung the large ornamental wheel to port, it eagerly answered the helm. The long disused but brightly painted rudder chains clanked and squealed in protest as they slowly travelled in and out along the polished deck to the rudderpost, turning the rudder and thereby guiding the large un-wielding vessel out into the river. Now free of the dock, the Polly Woodside urged on by the LARC now pushing forcefully against her starboard stern section, swung silently around with the tide to face down stream.

"Tim let go the towline and manoeuvred the LARC up under the bow, where once again, he picked up the re-located towline and again secured it to the rear bollard of the LARC before opening up the throttle once more. Taking up the strain once more, ever so slowly the 'Polly Woodside' overcame the pull of the tide and made its way slowly down stream towards the bay, Clifton Springs and tomorrow.

"On the way down the river, a fair bit of crunching and banging was experienced as the vessel made its way through the partially destroyed barricades. Luckily, this action served to scrape some of accumulated growth of barnacles and seaweed from its iron hull and no structural damage was done. Here and there a few local Ferals using improvised water craft, attempted to clamber aboard the moving vessel, however a new style of hair cut compliments of a razor-sharp sword, suggested that it was far safer back on the river.

"As the modern-day river police or security patrols did not have any AGVs with which to pursue them, there was nothing they could do, except fire a few ill-directed weakened laser bolts at the quickly moving shadow. Some frustrated groups standing on the many long disused docks or piers, simply shouted at the passing vessel, which having picked up steerage, speed quickly disappeared into the man-made mist and gloom, heading for the safety of the bay it was soon well beyond their reach.

"Once out in the main shipping channel and well clear of the Williamstown foreshore, on board the LARC Tim eased off the engine revs and as he pulled out of the way allowing the sailing vessel to glide silently past, he changed over with

Pete, who had already clambered down the Jacob's ladder and had dropped into the cargo well. Tim then proceeded to climb on-board the vessel. With Peter at the helm and now under power once more, the LARC moved up front and taking up the strain, continued towing the vessel further and further away from the darkened shoreline.

"Now on board, Tim went directly to the engine room and looked with delight at the site of the large caterpillar diesel marine engine he had only recently helped to install. Using a maintenance key, which was located in a secret compartment built into the ornate panelling, he opened the security gate designed to protect the engine from Ferals and unwanted attention, proceeded to check the oil level. After which, using a long metal bar fitted into one of the many holes in the flywheel, he manually primed the fuel system by barring the engine over a few times and once happy with it, he connected its bank of batteries and switched on the power. Finally, he turned on the igniters and when the glow plug light went out, hit the start button.

"Here in the long silent confines of the engine room, the resounding 'clack' of the starter motor solenoid engaging and the impatient hi-pitched whirring of the starter motor, as it turned the great engine faster and faster, was almost deafening. But to an engineer like Tim, what a sweet sound that great engine made as it fired and ran up to full revs before cutting back on the governor to idle. Grinning from ear to ear, he could not have been more pleased. Whilst down in the engine room he closed the circuit breakers turning on the electricity to lights and equipment and switched on the large refrigerators, which would be required to store cold and frozen foods on their arrival in Clifton Springs.

"Running up the companionway from the engine room, he made his way to the bow and called to Peter to come aboard, and while he originally intended to blow the LARC up, he just could not bring himself to do it… Besides, it was now almost out of fuel anyhow, so it would not be of much value to any one immediately, so, he called down to Peter to drop the tow and come up alongside the port side of the vessel and pass up all the boxes of fish eggs, fingerlings, crustation and fish food. Then leaving the engine running to use up the last bit of fuel, the LARC was pointed towards the bottom of Port Phillip Bay and the Werribee River. This done, on the last pass along the side of the vessel, Peter leapt onto the dangling Jacob's ladder and the faithful old LARC having done its job well, motored quietly into oblivion.

"With the engine now normalised, and the cooling water pump working okay, the revolutions were throttled back to idle and through a reduction gearbox and a manually operated clutch lever; the propeller drive was engaged, the clutch let out and the engine revs were built back up to 1800 per minute. Now well out in Port Phillip Bay, for the first time in over two centuries the 'Polly Woodside' under her own power surged forward on the greatest adventure of its life.

Now in control of the vessel, Tim relieved Dean at the helm, spun the helm over to starboard, un-caged the Gimbals compass and on a bearing roughly west by southwest, motored towards the far side of Port Phillip Bay: delighted at just how easy the large vessel handled the mild conditions. The bodies of the unfortunate Ferals, still lying where they had fallen on the deck, were now committed to the deep and several buckets of salt water; removed all evidence of their passing. As Peter and Dean commenced to open up the vessel ready to receive the anticipated cargo, an inspection of the vessel below decks revealed several female and juvenile Ferals still cowering in the dark confines of one of the cabins. As there was no alternative, it was decided that they would stay confined there until the vessel reached Clifton Springs.

"On deck, they opened the cargo hatches to allow fresh air into the holds, removed the heavy plastic side curtain from the rear of the vessel; creating a small-protective pen for the livestock on the unprotected front deck, also in the forward hold and sail compartment. Here the stock, although a little cramped, would at least be dry and safe from the anticipated severe weather conditions known to exist once the vessel was at sea. The fish, crustaceans and eggs, were secured and covered amid ships, while the food for them was stowed away below decks.

"Down below in the calm waters of the bay, as though they had been doing it all their lives, for the first time in their life bottle nosed and bay dolphins played and rode happily along on the bow wave created by the moving vessel. To the northwest, the outline of the You Yang's Mountains dominated the skyline, while away to the south the dark outlines of the Great Otway Ranges disappeared into the misty rain towards Cape Shanks.

"The fresh tangy-salty smell of the sea and a pale moon just visible through the drizzling rain, shone weakly through a halo of diffused light, creating a feeling long since lost to modern society. For Tim it was like old times…as tonight as the night flying petrels, silver backed gulls and grey mollymawks did like their ancestors before them; wheel back and forth diving in the wake of a moving vessel, searching for food in a century old ritual. The vibrant scene caused Tim's thoughts to stray to distant happier days when he and the family had spent many enjoyable hours fishing out here on the bay, water skiing, swimming or simply listening to the laughter of children playing in the shallows along the foreshore. A scene no longer enjoyed by the inhabitants of this vast environment friendly nation.

"As the grey light of the piccaninny dawn grew ever brighter, the outline of the Bellarine Peninsular stood proud and green on the south-western horizon while with a worried expression on his face, Tim wondered about everyone else, *Did everything go all right collecting the stores? Did they all make it safely to the jetty? Did they get Mum and Dad?*

"Although he was worried, he also knew that there was nothing more he could have done, the die was now cast, they were all committed, and somehow, they just had to be waiting. So absorbed was he in thoughts, that he forgot the most important thing when master of any vessel.

"'Look where you are bloody going,' as he was quickly jolted back to reality by Peter calling urgently from the bow cried. 'Debris dead ahead.'

"Sure enough, lying dead ahead of the vessel was the partly submerged wreckage of a large international A-G cargo vehicle. At that distance and their speed, it was too late to come about in either direction… If they did, all they could achieve would be to hit the wreckage side on bringing down the masts and yardarms, in which case their great adventure would be over before it even started. So, taking a gamble, he called out to Dean who was down in the engine room.

"'Hard astern, Dean, and when I tell you, go full ahead, okay.'

"Down below the engine went quiet for a moment or two before revving up again in reverse gear and pushing everyone forward, as the wreckage drew rapidly closer the reverse thrust took over and the bow of the vessel dipped down into the sea arresting its forward motion. Now only a short distance away, Tim frantically spun the helm to port, steering the vessel towards the lowest section of the partially submerged craft just forward of the bridge, which was awash with seawater.

"'Okay full ahead,' he called at the top of his voice. Once more, the vessel slowed slightly before lifting its bow to surge forward under full revs. The cavitation wave or swell following the vessel now passed through under the keel of the vessel and as the wave surged forward over the wreck, the 'Polly Woodside' rode up with it to pass safely over the partially submerged craft. A fair bit of banging and screeching was heard with some wobbling experienced as they passed over the wreckage, then silence. Behind them, the surface of the sea was covered with a swirling mass of accumulated seaweed, barnacles, muscles and marine growth, which had been scrapped from the hull of their vessel during the near impact.

"While the lapse in concentration had almost proved disastrous, the end result reduced the drag caused by the years of accumulated marine growth and dramatically improved handling and speed of the vessel. The engine revs were increased once more with no apparent vibration, which indicating no damaged propeller or a bent shaft. However, from that point on, the engine revolutions were reduced to three quarters ahead, which was about eight knots and Dean was stationed up in the bowsprit to act as lookout specifically for spotting any further debris."

Chapter 9
All Aboard

"As dense foliage now covered the landscape along the approaching dark and inhospitable looking shoreline, everything looked the same. The once popular little beach and playground at Clifton Springs was over grown, gone were the swings, slippery slides and Barbeques, nothing was recognisable any more. At Point Henry, far to his right, Tim could see the tall gaunt remains of Alcoa Australia – which in its hay day as a large aluminium processing plant. This giant alumna smelter once had a workforce of several thousand working three shifts, but now because it was suspected of giving the workers in the Pot-rooms and carbon rod plant, lung and kidney cancer as well as polluting the atmosphere; it too had been closed for many years. Finally, because it did not conform to the modern-day pollution standards, it now stood rusting away. A gaunt, yet defiant rusting epitaph to man's stupidity and short sightedness.

"Now and then, ahead and just off to the port side (left) of the vessel, the headlights of the convoy vehicles was seen flickering on and off brightly, guiding them in towards to the jetty. As the tide was on the ebb, the vessel being positioned on the northern western or left-hand side of the jetty was simply more by good luck than by good seamanship.

"As the jetty reached out towards them, Tim came about to port facing the bow northeast towards the main shipping channel and put the vessel into reverse, guiding it astern towards the shoreline. Every now and then allowing the engine to idle down, he allowed the vessel to drift slowly side on with the outgoing tide. Every now and then putting it into reverse to keep it square on to the jetty. Stern first he manoeuvred the large vessel in towards the shoreline. Finally, and with just a gentle bump, it drifted up too and came to rest against the port or left-hand side of the jetty.

"Ashore, many eager, excited and willing hands grabbed the new mooring lines thrown forward and aft quickly securing the vessel up against the jetty. First up, the remaining Ferals and their few scant possessions were brought up from down below and put ashore where Dean escorted them to the fringe of the forest, which lay just a short distance from the end of the jetty.

"In anticipation of those on board would secure the vessel, the vast collection of commodities: food, water, medical supplies, clothing and personal effects. Along with assorted fodder for the stock and seed for the poultry, which had been picked up from the nature reserve by the first available vehicle, had been stacked in two separate piles, one on the end and one in the centre of the jetty where the cargo holds on the vessel where known to be.

"Without need of shouted commands, the gang way was lowered over the side and re-pinned on its pivots and the stores and equipment commenced coming aboard to be dropped down to eager hands waiting in the forward, centre and rear holds. The heaviest of the equipment required last was loaded first in the bottom of the hold with the lighter and first required last in on top. Unfortunately, all this feverish activity on a very old jetty soon began to take its toll and suffering from years of council neglect, swayed and creaked under the load. Planking and odd pieces of decking began to fall away and splashed down into the quickening run of the outgoing tide. As they continued to load the vessel, the jetty now assailed not only by the weight of the cargo, but the gentle urgent bumping and movement of the heavy vessel affected by the quickening pace of the outgoing tide, increasingly moaned and complained louder and louder.

"At the entrance to the jetty, Dean stood with his arms folded and apparently totally at ease, yet his keen senses fully alert as he studied the surrounding undergrowth for any signs of activity or movement, but at this point there were none. It was apparent that the local Ferals had not been able to keep up with the vehicles as they had pushed their way through the almost impenetrable growth to reach the jetty. Finally, with exception of the small collection of livestock, everything to come aboard was now safely stowed away and the hatch covers fitted; they had almost completed their task. However, as the livestock seemed to fear the rickety, old jetty, putting them on board became very time consuming as in a vain attempt to escape, the animals ran and jumped at everyone and everything in their path.

"Then, just as they were running out of time to catch the last of the run of the ebb tide, two of the young female Ferals that had been recently put ashore when the vessel first arrived, suddenly re-appeared out of the scrub. Talking to the animals in a strange manner, like a 22nd century version of Noah and the Ark, they led them up too and along the jetty to the side of the vessel where one by one they were lifted up and carried quickly onboard. It would seem that living on the fringe of society for many decades, that these strange people of the forest could control the animals in a manner quite unknown to the modern society. Finally, when only the two young rams remained, the girls clung to them and gestured towards the vessel…it was quite apparent that they were begging to come.

"'What do you reckon, Dad,' Tim said turning to his father who was already busy laying out the maps and charts he had kept all these years as souvenirs.

"'Well,' Ivan said looking up and surveying the scene. 'They certainly have a way with the stock that is for sure and when we arrive at our destination that same stock will require people to shepherd them up into the Red River area Macquarie Island is still a nature reserve you realise, we just can't let them run wild you know.'

"'Okay, bring. Let them come aboard and they can help look after the flock,' and turned once more to study the charts.

"'Dean,' Tim shouted to the lone figure of his son, standing between the vessel and the forest, 'come on, bring them on board.'

"Once they were all on board, Tim looked at the two young women of unknown age standing there locked in one another's arm and said slowly, nodding and gesturing towards the forward sail compartments.

"'Alright you can come, but until we get out onto the open sea and we can find something better for you to wear, for the time being you are to stay with the flock; they will be your responsibility.'

"'A daily ration of food and water will be supplied for you and you are to keep the area as clean as you can, do you understand?' The furtive looks from left to right and towards the sail locker indicated that they understood quite well, what was said and after a nod from Tim, like the primitive children they were, they scurried up forward to disappear down into the sail locker. Then suddenly after all the desperate preparations, it was now time to go!

"'Let go forward,' Tim called while swinging the helm hard over to port and as he watched the hawser being pulled in, called down to Dean in the engine room, 'half ahead.' With the vessel under power once more and the stern still secured to the now rapidly collapsing jetty, it caused the bow of the vessel to slowly come away to port. And as it cleared the timberwork, Tim called, 'Let go the stern line.' However, as there was no one left ashore to untie it, it was simply thrown into the sea. Neutralising the helm, Tim called, 'full ahead,' and clearing the jetty the 'Polly Woodside' underway once more, headed out into deep water towards the main channel and into the history books.

"'Come about to starboard Tim,' Ivan said, and run parallel to the main channel until we reach the swing basin where it where it curves south towards Port Arlington, we aren't drawing enough water to worry about running aground.' Calling the adult men and cadets' males together, Tim left the navigation to Ivan and the helm to Matthew, the former merchant navy officer and now senior coxswain for the voyage to head along the deck and check the sail fixtures and riggings. In addition, to explain to the deck crew the names of the sails and riggings, what they were used for and more importantly, what he expected of them once they hit the open sea. Until then, as there was no time to raise the sails and learn how to tack and control such a large vessel in confined, quickly moving waters like these, so for the time being the vessel would stay under power. There would be ample time and room to teach them how to dress the vessel once it reached the safety of the open sea.

"Down below in the galley and cabin areas, the older women and girls set about cleaning the area and putting the galley and what living quarters there were, in order. The men, girls and boys not attending sailing briefing armed with hammers and cold chisels, set about removing a large riveted metal panel separating the galley from No1 Hold by chiselling off the retaining rivets. Once access was gained, they commenced to build additional sleeping accommodation or bunks along the walls of the holds on above the top of the cargo.

"As the 'Polly Woodside' was never intended to be a passenger-carrying vessel, but a cargo ship, apart from the four main cabins, recently installed by misguided enthusiast, there were no original sleeping quarters. So extra bunks had to be constructed and were fitted around the walls of the holds, both above and on the cargo. During the voyage, the older women and men, the captain, first officer and navigator would sleep in the main cabins, while everyone else was all in together in the temporary hold accommodation, it was neither the time nor the place to be prude.

"For some degree of privacy, the female cadets would work out shower rosters. The men and boys would shower on deck in the mornings, while later in the day, when everyone should be on deck watch or asleep, the females would bathe up forward.

"Under the watchful eyes of Peter and Dean, the deck hands were shown how to check and service the vessels salt-water intake and bilge pumps. The bilge was pumped dry and the ballast tanks pumped full to stabilise the vessel. The many plastic containers of drinking water, which had been brought on board, were counted and safely stored. To stop them chaffing or rubbing together and causing them to leaking during anticipated violent weather they would encounter, layers of soft insulation was packed between them. In addition, as there was no desalination system or condensers on board, a daily water ration per head had to be worked out. The older women were responsible for making an inventory of the food supplies required for the journey and to prepare a daily menu. To see them safely to their destination, they also had to create a ration scale, from the allocated food stocks for the voyage which would have to be strictly adhered too.

"Ivan suggested that they should push out into Bass Strait, then west across the Great Australian Bight towards the tip of Western Australia to the south east of Rottenness Island. Where, turning their back to the great westerly trade winds would curve down along the great navigational arc through the roaring forties into the furious fifties, a thousand nautical miles and more to the south-south east. Also, that the wet weather gear already stored on-board for the original volunteer deck crews, should be broken out and issued to the new deck crews.

"In the calm waters of the bay and before they reached Port Phillip Heads, everything required to close up the vessel ready for the open sea had to be completed as best they could. Riggings were checked and secured; down in the sail locker pushing a few sheep to one side, new sails were brought up to replace any suspect ones, which were then folded and stored away. The many dozens of various double and triple pulley blocks or sheave wheels located high up in the riggings were removed and dismantled. The rollers and pins greased, riggings re-run through them and the blocks rebuilt to stop them seizing under load and also to make it easier on the deck crew when hauling the heavy sails aloft or swinging the yardarms about. The new sails were then manually hauled aloft onto and made fast to the yardarms.

"Cargo hatches were covered with spare sailcloth or canvas and battened down to make them watertight, while the safety fence erected around the deck was checked and tightened. Finally, the rudder chains, which previously lay exposed along the stern deck from the helm to the rudderpost, were greased and lubricated and to stop getting feet or legs entangled in them in turbulent seas they were encased in a false box or cover.

"Shipboard chores that the adventurers could never have imagined in their wildest dreams being part of, suddenly became not only a reality but also an everyday occurrence. For some, except on the computer internet they had never even seen a sailing ship, let alone try to sail a real one. Now however, their very lives and the lives of a new generation depended on them learning and learning quickly.

"Everything ship shape for the moment, the voyage towards the heads unfolded in the misty light of a new day and the entire compliment, well with the exception of those on duty found time to line the deck rails and watched the foreshore of the Bellarine Peninsular gliding silently past in the distance. Sadly, with the exception of the older adults, it was to be the first and last time that they would ever see it.

Most had been born and lived within the protection of an unrealistic environmentalist's dream, where everything other than the human race, had lorded over the sea and the land.

"Now they were amazed at the different sounds and noises they were experiencing, the bubbling laughter of the sea as it raced past the hull, hissing and whispering many long-held secrets of life and colour. The strange inviting sounds of a vessel now so alive and vibrant; the tangy smell of salt water and behind the vessel, the poetry and motion of the various species of seabird now gliding back and forth in the light misty rain.

"To the elderly who could remember the scene as it once was, it was goodbye forever to a former way of life, a civilisation they once known and loved. To the young, it was the beginning of a fascinating voyage into another world. A life beyond tomorrow, and the beginning of a new way of life.

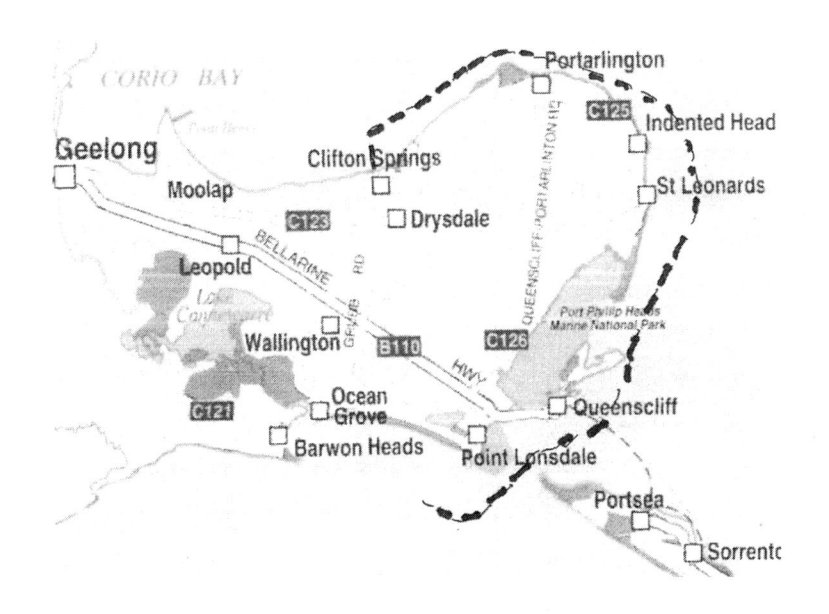

Chapter 10
Beyond The Horizon

"Deep within the bowls of the vessel, pushing it relentlessly along hour after hour at a steady eight knots, the reassuring pulsing throb, throb, throbbing of the great caterpillar engine propelled them on towards Port Arlington, Indented Heads, St Leonard's, Queens cliff, Point Lonsdale, The Rip, Bass Strait and the endless Southern Ocean beyond…was music to their ears.

"As they approached the heads, here and there along the way, they passed many primitive canoes containing feral groups or families from different localities along the Bellarine Peninsular; fishing the out run of the tide.

"At the mouth of the rip and on the bottom of the ebb tide, the 'Polly Woodside' passed by the long since decommissioned lighthouse at Point Lonsdale…a lighthouse, which now stood silent and deserted. No Aldis lamp blinked out a message of farewell and to mark their departure, no one lowered and raised the funny looking new flag, which somehow we just had to have.

"Passing out through the heads, the 'Polly Woodside' dipped her bow down into the rolling easterly swell of the incoming tide, which now had begun to roll in through the narrow passage in the rip and lifted up over the turbulent incoming swell. As though bracing her for the battle, which lay ahead, the gallant little vessel shuddered slightly at that first violent impact and as in days of old, nonchalantly cast the incoming sea aside.

"Once clear of the turbulence at the entrance to Port Phillip Bay, Ivan ordered the coxswain to come about south by southeast. Heeding the order shouted back by Tim, the first officer, the newly appointed coxswain spun the helm to the starboard and the vessel heeled over slightly as it came about onto the new heading. As the great sailing vessel motored further and further out to sea south by southeast, mile after nautical mile slide quietly bye beneath her keel. Coming about south by southwest she slowly but surely motored out to sea leaving the mainland of Australia far behind until finally, with the blink of an eye, the Australian coastline was no longer visible.

"With the evening breeze off the east-southeast quarter and with a long low, easy swell running, the engine rpms were dropped to idle, just enough to allow the vessel to make way and not wallow between troughs in the swell, and also to allow the engine time to cool and normalise.

"On deck, the main sails, along with forward, centre and aft. The four forward jibs, six topsails, two aft topsails and two stern sheets were all hoisted. At the end of that first hectic day from pulling on the ropes to haul the madly flapping sails taut or to swing the yardarms about the crew both young and old alike, sported a rather good selection of blisters on their soft hands. These were the first, but definitely not the last time they were too experienced many such large angry looking red blisters on their tender hands.

"With the 'Polly Woodside' now fully dressed and flying a wardrobe of seventeen sails, the yardarms were swung about across the wind and as the remaining sails were reefed in tight and catching the wind, she heeled further over to starboard and for the first time in almost two centuries made way under her own power. Once the driveline was neutralised and the engine normalised, it was shut down.

"On deck, the silence broken only by the creaking of the aged hull, mingled with the humming vibrations of the taut straining riggings, and the shivering rustle of the sails was almost over powering. As the mournful whispering sighs of the night wind vibrated through the riggings, it created a scene unlike anything they had ever experienced. It was an opera set to music by Mother Nature as a final curtain call to a former way of life and the herald of a new and exciting one, that whispered to them that they were now all alone and in God's hands.

"As there is no electronic gadgetry on board the vessel to require the services of a technician, Wayne had devoted this first day to listing everyone on board and working out a crew roster. Each and every one of the younger generations, boys and girls, as well as the younger adults were paired off to work together controlling the topsails. While down below at deck level, along with the deck crew, the older generation would attend to the everyday running of the vessel.

"Ivan would be the captain and navigator. Tim would be the first officer, while Mitta Moody was ships engineer and second officer, with Barry MacFarlane and Rob the Doctor as catering officers.

"There would be three bosons, each of whom would be responsible for the vessel during each shift. They would be

Peter, Alan and Dean, with Wayne as sail master. Finally, Alvario, Lisa's dad; a master carpenter/cabinet maker, would be shipwright or carpenter responsible for the maintenance and overall condition of the vessel. Working with the Doc as the nutritional guide it fell to the older women to control below decks, where on a large oil stove they were also responsible for cooking meals to coincide with various shift changes, maintain a strict ration scale as well as looking after the hygiene and cleanliness of the accommodation.

"As darkness set in that first evening, with all the shipboard duties allocated, the ancient vessel now under control, steadily made way under its own power. As evening settled down for the last time the deck was checked. The riggings securing the yardarms were let out to allow the mainsails to balloon out a little thereby taking the strain off the old masts. All loose rigging lines were coiled and secured away, or made fast over marlin spikes or tied in neat coils along the deck railing. On their first night at sea, indeed a very hungry and exhausted crew retired to the friendly, inviting but somewhat crowded warmth below decks for a well-earned meal.

"Dinner that evening consisted of freshly baked lamb killed and dressed early that afternoon along with roast vegetables, with the dinner complimented with red and white wine. For dessert, tinned fruits and hot homemade custard followed by freshly cooked scones and jam, it was indeed a memorable occasion. Combined with the aroma of tangy spices and fresh food cooking, the galley was a smorgasbord of mouth-watering odours the young ones had never before experienced yet instantly loved.

"After dinner, for those who were not on duty it was a turn around the deck under a mantle of stars, or lean over the railing and watch with fascination the ever-changing swirling phosphorus bubbles creating weird and wonderful patterns of blue and gold in dark waters of Bass Strait now rushing, hissing past on its eternal journey. Finally, to bed… where rocked to sleep by the gentle rolling motion of the great sailing ship, they drifted off not only to sleep, but to a new and challenging way of life.

"Now well out to sea the rain, which the adventurers had become accustom to for the greater part of their lives…ceased. Moreover, as the evening shadows deepened, the cloud cover opened up and for the first time in their short lives, those on deck, looked up at a heaven now full of brilliant, twinkling stars: the saucepan, the bear, the big dipper, and the Southern Cross, to the west the bright evening star and above a galaxy of constellations. Tonight, with only the wind whistling through the riggings and the occasional flapping of the sails to break the feeling of eternal silence, there was no pitta-patter of constant rain, no idle chatter from a radio, TV or entertainment console. Tonight, with just the sound of the wind, the light from a million stars and a large lover's moon now peeping cautiously over the northeaster horizon; it was indeed a sobering, tranquil moment.

"For those clustered around the helm, listening to the wind, watching the movement of the sea and learning how to hold the great vessel across the wind or keeping it on course via the large gimbals compass. A compass, which swung back and forth and from side to side, yet all the while laying perfectly flat and level in it great brass and glass covered case, was an evening to remember.

"During that first evening, the selected coxswains took turns at the wheel keeping the vessel on course and feeling for the slightest wind shift, and when one did occur, urged on by the shift boson calling for the sails to be let out or closed up the novice crew reacted keenly. Alternatively, the yardarms to be swung about to take the strain off the old masts and yardarms, the crew learning quickly how to bring the vessel back into the wind while still remaining on course.

"Night passed without incident and the following morning, while the vessel had not made much distance during the night, dawn saw them standing well out to sea beyond Portland in southern Victoria with each member of the deck crew just a little more confident in his or her ability to control the vessel. With the Poly Woodside now running easily before a moderate northeasterly wind at eight knots, and the fact they had not slept for almost 48 hours Tim and Ivan, along with those trainees not required on deck had a warm meal and on hitting their bunks, dropped quickly off into an exhausted sleep.

"Without any major hassles, the routine of running and dressing such a large vessel fell quickly into place. Those adults with previous mechanical skills quickly regained them, while those who had never seen anything like this before in their lives, learnt quickly and willingly, sometimes with over-powering enthusiasm.

"Over the next few days, they cleared the south-east coast of Australia and came about west-southwest between Tasmania and Victoria into Bass Strait. After passing to the north of Tasmania, which now lay to the south of their course, they set course along the South Australian border and into the Great Australian Bight. Late one afternoon in fair weather and good winds, they came upon many large schools of blue fin tuna, the torpedoes of the sea, which were accompanied by many species of surface feeding fish. Untouched by commercial fishing over the centuries, these vast schools of fish, were feeding on a multitude of small surface feeding baitfish attracted to the safety of the ship, causing the surface of the ocean around them to boil in a feeding frenzy.

"The recently acquired strong fishing lines were hastily brought up from down below, and once fitted with colourful spinners or large baited hooks, were quickly attached to the new rods or any long poles they could lay their hands on and were hurriedly dropped over the side. In an intense feeding frenzy, many hundreds of large tuna, albacore, barracuda, mackerel and other surface feeding species were hauled aboard. By dusk, as the sun hung tenaciously on the western horizon, the fishing stopped, the huge catch had been bled, gutted and the decks washed down. That part of today's catch not required for immediate use were salted down and stored away to relieve the pressure on the limited supply of fresh meat and other rations, or simply set aside to be used later.

"For the youngsters the thrill of catching a fish for the first time in their life was an exhilarating experience. That evening, for those sitting up in the bow of the vessel with a parcel of fresh fish and crisp chips doused with vinegar, pepper and salt, or for those dinning in the galley on freshly steamed or baked fish, was not only a great new treat and an evening to remember, it also created a bonding process amongst them. The pushing and shoving, along with along with the odd nervous laughter and giggles of both boys and girls cuddled up together in the bow of the vessel seeking protection from the cool evening breeze, created an intimate scene; Indeed, a far cry from a sterile brassy entertainment system of yesterday.

"The following morning the sea around the vessel was still buzzing with piscatorial activity, and it was hard to say whether it was a nutrient upheaval or simply an overabundance of plankton and krill. Whatever it was, it certainly had drawn large shoals of fish, both large and small to the area. Once more, the lines and lures from the fishing poles were cast over the side and the fish commenced coming on board once more, soon the deck ran red with blood as fish after fish came up over the side.

"Some of these magnificent Tuna weighing in excess of 150-200 lbs and were more than one person or in fact two people could handle, so the eager fisherman worked in pairs two to a rod. In their excitement, the flapping bleeding fish, the blood and disgorged food running back and forth across the polished deck something bad was sure to happen!

"And, sadly it did.

"Two of the female cadets, Rhoma and Lauda who always worked and in fact did most things together, hooked onto a large tuna and as they fought desperately to bring it up over the gunnels, someone came to their aid with a long gaff to help pull it onboard. However, in the heat of battle, the laughter and the shouting, the vessel hit by a freak wave heeled suddenly over to port as it dipped down into a trough. As it came up, the vessel suddenly heeled over to starboard …the helper fell against them and both girls still clutching the rod losing their footing on the bloodied, slippery deck and disappeared over the side.

"All over the vessel, the cry that sent a shiver down everyone's spine was clearly heard.

"'Man overboard.'

"Hearing the cry for help, Tim ordered the coxswain to come about into the waves and as the vessel lost way, he ordered the sails to be reefed. The engine was started and the vessel once in gear began to systematically search the area in an ever-increasing arc. They circled the area repeatedly looking for any sign of the girls, but as the sun began to sink, search as they may, all hope of finding them alive had passed.

"Was it possible that they had become tangled in the line and been taken down into the depths by such a large fish or had they been taken by one of many great white sharks, which had recently been sighted following the vessel, feeding on this same school of fish? This first tragic encounter with death left a lasting impression on the younger members who had never before experience death in any shape or form, let alone witness such a brutal loss of close friends first hand. A simple ceremony, a few well-chosen words and they were left with a fleeting sketchy memory of two vibrant young women that some had known for just a few short weeks.

"As the 'Polly Woodside' prepared to departed the area, a sombre mood fell over the vessel, the rippling spontaneous giggles and laughter, the pushing and friendly jostling of the younger set was not heard as often as in the past few hectic weeks; sadly, they all seemed to have grown up so very quickly. With a heavy heart, Ivan had ordered the vessel to come about onto their original heading, the sails were let go and set once more and on picking up steerage the engine was shut down, and under its own power the vessel made way once more.

"What really happened, would they ever know?

"However, unsecured pole fishing over the side was never under taken again so lightly. As though everything had been for a reason, the loss of the two female cadets opened the door to the two feral girls. Their coming and going from the forward sail locker indicated that they were taking food and water down to their charges, exercising them on deck and cleaning the area and of an evening, would come up on deck to eat the meals brought up for them.

"They were shy furtive creatures, almost primitive in their ways, after years of neglect their hair was matted and fused together. Their apparel consisting of odd assorted bits of clothing, which they had either found or stolen over the years, were mere rags. With each passing day, as the 'Polly Woodside' sailed further and further across the Great Australian Bight, the sea becoming much rougher and the air temperature dropping noticeably. It obvious that the two feral girls would have to be quickly integrated into this unique community, for as the conditions worsened left to their own devices outside they would not survive the voyage. This task of integration was allotted to Lisa and Sharyn; the latter in her late years was a country girl at heart, outwardly a rough diamond but with a heart of gold. While Alvario's daughter and Dean's wife, Lisa, was a very educated woman and a mother who had the ability to gain their confidence quickly.

"To break down the language and social barrier was no easy task, but with each passing day, using the wildlife as a central talking point, the girls slowly gained their confidence and conversations grew longer and longer as they began to re-gain the fundamentals of the Australian language. The introduction to a shower was not so simple; they shunned the idea as though their lives depended on it. It was apparent to their mentors that they were afraid to take their clothing off for fear of losing it. Although new clothing were laid out and explained to them, they were confused with the brassiere and small lace knickers. Warm woollen spencers and skivvies to replace the battered old UV protective clothing and home-made leather attire, which in this cool climate was no longer of any value to them. It was only natural, that as they had never seen this type of clothing in their lives, they simply refused to touch it.

"What to do with them that was the question? They could not be left where they were, forcible manhandle, or anything that would defeat the effort to introduce them into this unique community. At a round table conference, it was agreed that as they had to be brought inside, the only way was to sedate them with their dinner. Then whilst they were asleep, Robbin the doctor, after their rotting garments had been removed and bathed by the older women, would give them a complete medical and assisted by Ron the dentist, clean up their teeth and mouth where required.

Once washed and their medical examination completed, they would then leave them to the women who would cut their lank matted hair. Their long fingernails and toe nails and dress them completely from the underwear up. With everyone in agreement, the following evening as the sun sank low on the western horizon, as the two Feral girls sat up in the bow eating their dinner and watching a school of dolphin playing down there on the bow wave, slowly but surely the tranquilliser took effect and they dropped off into a deep sleep.

"With little time to spare, they were carried below and the older women divested them of the rough clothing and gently bathed them. With except of their matted hair and rapier-like fingernails, which could do you a serious physical injury; physically they were in good condition. Their matted hair was bobbed like the old, short back and sides and their long toenails, which had actually grown back underneath their toes, were cut and shaped. A dusting of fresh talcum powder and deodorant were applied, and then while some of the older women stayed, the doctor gave them quick medical. Strange as it may seem, medically they were very clean, with no apparent skin or cancerous disorders caused by their constant exposure to the much-published UV levels and except for a few odd scars or spear marks; they were medically fit. Stranger still, both were still virgins, which indicated a strong moral fibre within their family group or clan.

"The medical and dental check complete, a series of immunisation shots and the insertion of a medical sensor chip in their buttock completed the medical and doc left them in the care of the women to dress. Once dressed from underclothes to heavy serviceable outer clothing they were returned to the bow of the vessel and seated in the same positions, as they were before they had gone to sleep. Awakening to a new life, the girls slowly pushed back the blanket covering them and stretched like two wild sensuous native cats awakening from a deep sleep.

"As they looked at one another slowly but surely their transformation dawned on them. They ran their manicured fingers through their hair and probably for the first time, admired one another's clean washed faces. They rubbed their arms and their bottoms where the injections and a chip had been inserted and looked furtively about the vessel to see if they were being observed. However, apart from the crew on the yardarm going about their business climbing up and down the riggings, or balancing on the swaying yardarms far above the deck, no one, it seemed, showed the slightest interested in them.

"Having won their confidence with small gifts; a mirror in which to see themselves, feminine things they had never seen before such as lace handkerchiefs and pretty shawls. The girls were eventually introduced below decks and given a shared berth out of the weather. Weather that with each passing day was becoming progressively colder and the sea rougher. As the weeks passed quickly by, the feral girls were now fully integrated and accepted into the small community. Each of these girls, using well-documented yet unwritten age-old feminine wiles, had very quickly secured themselves boyfriends, to whit Aub and Dominic, who, although not allowed to touch, were never left to stray too far from sight.

"Like a great migrating hump back whale, the 'Polly Woodside' finally reached a furthermost point southwest across the Great Australian Bight to a position approximately 20 nautical miles below Rottenness Island. There, coming about to port the yardarms were swung across the vessel to starboard and catching the westerly trade winds, the vessel heeling over to port and taking up the strain once more she was committed south by the trade winds into the roaring forties and later the furious fifties. Following the great navigational arc like so many great wool clippers, square-rigged sailing vessels, and brigantines of yesteryear, with the roaring forties, blowing of Cape of Good Hope at her back 'The Polly Woodside' ran ahead of the strong westerly wind down across the Indian Ocean towards the South Pacific Ocean and the Antarctic Continent.

"By providing them with mostly fine days and clear blue skies, it seemed to the intrepid travellers that Mother Nature was riding with them. While at the same time creating an opera of moving, living colour as day after day various species of wandering, royal, black brow and grey-headed albatross, large southern giant and northern giant macronette's hali petrels, light mantled sooty albatross and sooty shearwaters. Along with Mother Carey's Chickens, dove prion's, assorted petrels and mutton birds continually swept back and forth behind the vessel. While now and then, large schools of flying fish would break the surface of the sea to go winging their way across the waves for a great distance before splashing back into the waiting sea.

"Slight to medium winds with only the occasional squall, which caused them to quickly reef the Mainsle's and run on small amidship's jibs for steerage, seemed to be the order of the day. When the wind was down and it was safe to go on deck mixed bathing under the salt-water showers created fun and games as well as personal bonding between the younger set. It was as though Mother Nature had already mysteriously segregated the group, drowning couples together as they unconsciously begun to pair off for protection and a lifetime together.

"As the weather for the most part were simply light blustering squalls, which meant occasionally reefing the odd sail now and then for short periods it added little or no drama to the long voyage. Days of watching the never-ending panorama and spectacle of wandering albatross, black brow, grey headed and sooty albatross, along with many varieties of petrels; pintadoo petrels, shearwaters and prions that swung back and forth behind the vessel in search of food, came and went quickly as the weeks turned into months. Then finally, on the 10th day of July 2150, a long 340 years since the day it was first discovered, there on the eastern horizon a short distance ahead at 54 degrees 34 minutes south, 158 degrees 57 minutes east was the outline of a large green island.

"'Land Ahoy,' ten points off the port bow called the lookout. They had finally reached Macquarie Island. The old ANARE expeditioner had come home.

Yes, the 'Polly Woodside' had done her job well and now as in those days long gone; the great sailing vessel was once more alive with running, climbing figures as the crew skilfully made their way up into the riggings ready to reef the sails. They were so excited you would think the greenies had given them permission to chop down a few trees to save their house from being burnt down or flattened by falling branches. But no, it was the thrill of the un-expected, most of them thought they would never see land again and like the fabled flying Dutchman of yore, were forever doomed to sail the seven seas, never finding a homeport.

"'Yes… looking bleak and very inhospitable, Macquarie Island, standing proud and defiant in a sea of endless proportions, appeared out of the mist of time. The intrepid voyagers were finally home."

Chapter 11
Macquarie Island

Macquarie Island @latitude 54°34 'South.

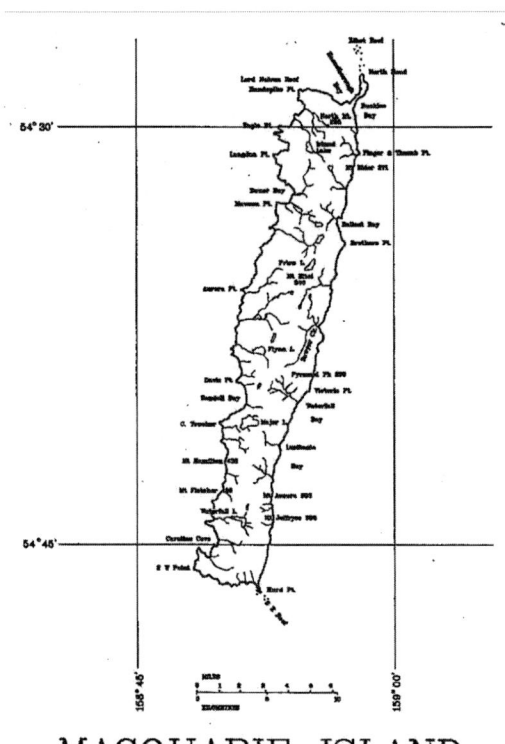

MACQUARIE ISLAND

(Looking down on the station from North Head shows the living quarters. The large building in the centre (1) is the mess joined to the hospital (2). Behind it is (3) the 16 room Sleeping area designated 'The Southern Aurora' and (4) the powerhouse south of it. Left under the arrow & green Knoll are the water tanks and behind (2) are the 16-room living quarters. The (5) ladies or married quarters in almost centre bottom with peak roof with store huts and Sealers Chapel along with several small huts and the large drive-in bulk store and refrigerators, is out of sight on right hand side of the picture then the OIC's quarters and fort Knox's 6. (7) Are the stables. The centre shows the isthmus with the radome and workshops with Buckles Bay to the right and Hassle borough Bay to the left, beyond and at the end of the isthmus is the razor back ridge leading up to the fog bound southern plateau. (At this time, the seal fence was not erected).

"Their future home, set right in the path of the great westerly winds and depressions, which blow continuously around the bottom of the Earth from the Cape of Good Hope to Cape Horn, is the only island or land mass at this latitude. With no other landmass in its path for thousands of nautical miles to impede their progress, these savage winds blow unabated across the island, year in and year out.

"Declared a wildlife sanctuary in 1933, Macquarie Island is approximately 25 miles long by 3.5 to 5 miles wide at the widest part, but only a few hundred feet wide at the narrowest part on the isthmus, as it is known on the northern end of the island. A fragile conglomerate, the island is the result of a volcanic upheaval rising up from the ocean floor many centuries ago and supports a continuous mountain range running its entire length, which rise at times from the lofty, barren plateau region to a height of 1500 feet above sea level.

"The island, laying half-way between Australia and Antarctic Continent stands as a lone sentinel guarding the approaches to that great frozen continent. Today, with the low cloud and ghostly fingers of fog and mist streaming from its lofty peaks, the island standing alone and so majestic in a sea of endless proportions, was indeed an awesome sight.

"Experiencing winds, which at times can exceed 100-130 miles per hour, that whip up giant seas and thundering waves, which crash endlessly ashore on the western side of the island, it is one shoreline that is rarely approached. But then again, with vessels under sail experiencing a sudden severe wind change, the eastern side of the island can be just as dangerous.

There are no natural harbour or jetty here and most landings made from some distance offshore were originally made on the eastern foreshore at Buckles Bay, Lusitania Bay and Hurd Point. Firstly, in six-oared long boats or cutters, then motorised longboats. In the early 1950s during the initial scientific years, landings were made from rubber pontoons, then later by amphibious craft and finally long-range helicopters. Finally, during the last years of occupation by the Antarctic Division, by large long-range jet-ranger helicopters, which serviced the island whilst the re-supply vessel was still far out to sea. Then, finally yet importantly, in this the 22nd century, anti-gravitational space vehicle.

"Just after the turn of the 22nd century due to the environmental policy of the day, the station here was closed down. However, it remained on the air as solar-powered automatic weather station, transmitting regular weather data and under maritime law, was always stocked with the necessary provisions to support a large contingent of cast-a ways or tourist, should an AGV or interplanetary craft crash in this area.

"When Tim's dad served here for two years as the officer in charge of two scientific expeditions on different occasions, he had often spoken of a small, secluded bay called Smugglers Cove. This was located right behind the living quarters on the eastern side under North Head called Garden Cove; this cove was used as an alternative-landing place by the sealers as far back as 1810. The existence of this small cove intrigued Tim and although useless to large sailing vessels of that era, today with a relatively shallow draught and a powerful diesel engine to aid manoeuvring, it may now be navigable by the 'Polly Woodside'.

"After many months at sea, sighting the island was an exciting moment. The youngsters, now more like young adults, scrambling up any available section of rigging, while down below, the adults lined the railings and looked somewhat apprehensively at the large, green, uninhabited landmass now looming up quickly.

"Each and every one of us, now actually confronted with our future home, while very excited, must also been having doubts or misgivings about it all. However, for one person, Ivan, the oldest of the group it was like coming home. Gone were the days of being cooped up in an old folk's home just waiting for God. Once more, he was master of the situation, Captain of this vessel and leader of a new community. Yes, it seemed that after all these years, the green tussock covered mist-shrouded walls of Macquarie Island had finally beckoned him home.

"As he stood there by his son, looking back in time, Tim rubbed his shoulders and enquired, 'are you alright, Dad?'

"'Yes, Tim, I am fine!' he replied.

'There are a lot of memories out there, a lot of laughter, yet a lot of heartbreak, it is something I never thought that I would see again.'

"'Never mind about me,' he quipped taking a deep breath, 'where are those charts of the island? We are about to need them now.'

"'The way the sea is rising,' he suggested, 'I feel we would be better off running down the West Coast, pass east around Bishop and Clerk Isles to the south, then turn back north into the wind along the eastern seaboard. That way we will have the wind on our port quarter and can stand off in the lee of the island while we decide where to put ashore, okay.'

"'Right'o, Dad. I mean, Aye, aye, Captain,' Tim replied with a wiry grin.

"It was plain to see that his father was revelling in the challenge. Once more with the challenge of a new life and the adventure that lay ahead, he was free and so alive. By early afternoon, while lying approximately one nautical mile off the western side of the island for steerage and safety, the vessel safely cleared Bishop and Clerk Islets, which lay at the end of an exposed submarine reef several nautical miles due south of the southern end of the island. The vessel, now came about and tacked north across the breeze. Driven ahead of the wind, as she ploughed her way valiantly north, like so many of her predecessors, the 'Polly Woodside', made a majestic sight on the vast expanse of Southern Ocean, an ocean long devoid of any vessel.

"It was obvious even to the uninitiated that the island extending from north to south was simply a vast mountainous, volcanic extrusion with seventeen-named mountain pushing up into the fog and cloud cover some 1500 feet or more. Today as in years gone by, long lazy, beckoning fingers of fog and mist, swirling from these lofty peaks, drifted east out over the South Pacific Ocean, twisting and curling like so many ghostly fingers beckoning the weary travellers home or to the unwary…their doom.

"Up past Hurd Point, Lusitania Bay, Green Gorge, Sandy Bay and the Nuggets, they sailed, until finally they came upon large seaweed-encrusted buoy anchored in Buckles Bay on the eastern side of the isthmus. This isthmus, was simply a long, sandy tussock grass-covered, mud and seal wallow section of low-lying land. It links North Head, which is simply a large volcanic conglomerate at the northern tip of the island, to the high plateau region of the main southern body of the island via a steep ascending razor back ridge, which rises abruptly from sea level in the centre of the southern end of the isthmus.

"'All Hands to the sails.'

"'Reef and furl the topsails, fore and aft jibs,' Tim called to the boson in charge. The deck crew galvanised into action by the shouted commands, quickly forgot their daydreaming and climbed high into the swaying riggings to secure the sails, on yardarms that had been swung about out of the wind. The engine was re-started and as the remaining Mainsles were now hauled away and secured, the propeller drive was engaged once more. Aloft, amongst the maze of ropes and riggings, the crewmembers finally hauled the large Mainsles up onto the yardarms where once folded, was clewed and tied off securely. Once opposite Buckles Bay and the narrow, sandy isthmus beneath North Head, the 'Polly Woodside' slowly hove too and slowly came about to the west.

"As the vessel idled up towards the buoy, a very small dinghy, known as the ships dory or painter was lowered over the side. On board, Peter accompanied by two of the cadets, Ron and Barry rowed to the bobbing, wallowing buoy trailing a strong hawser to attach as a mooring line to one of the many large, rusty weed and guano-encrusted rings, which were welded to the sides of the moving, twisting buoy.

"As though playing with them, the buoy, as it bobbed up and down, twisting and turning with each passing wave, easily resisting their frantic efforts to attach the hawser. Finally, using a long grappling pole with a hook attached, Ron managed to grab hold of it, pulling the dory up alongside and while hanging onto it for dear life, Barry, leaning well forward managed to clip the heavy metal karabiner spliced to the end of the hawser to one of the welded rings, making the line fast.

"Battling to hold the dory into the oncoming waves, Peter pulled hard on the oars trying in vain to keep the frail little craft heading into the oncoming waves. Unfortunately, the sheer weight of both boys in the bow of the little craft caused it dip below the waves and ship water. The sea rushed merrily in over the gunwales and in a few short minutes, the little craft disappeared beneath the waves. Now thrown into the freezing turbulent water, the three men were suddenly fighting for their lives.

"Watching from the Polly Woodside, Tim called to the coxswain to go astern, taking up the slack in the mooring line. Ivan, remembering a similar incident years before when on different occasions two of his men had fallen from the deck of the MV Nella Dan, into the sea, watched the scene unfold with horror. He knew very well that the longer they remained in the freezing cold water the smaller their chances of survival were. Although they were swimming strongly towards the vessel, he knew that they would only survive for three or four minutes in the freezing water. He knew that those down there in the freezing waters were now fighting for their very lives.

"'Tim,' he shouted, 'get the deck crew to throw lifebuoys with ropes attached to them, if they get washed in close to the shoreline, they will get tangled in the kelp field and drown.'

"Fortunately, the men down in the water were now only matter yards from the vessel and they eagerly grabbed the lifebuoys, which had fallen within their reach. Pulling them in against the hull, the deck crew helped them up the Jacob's ladders, which had been hurriedly lowered down the lee side of the vessel. Once back onboard, they were immediately rushed down below deck and placed in a hastily contrived bath of warm water to thaw out. To prevent the sudden shock of the hot water doing more harm than good as the warmth penetrated their cold wet clothing and their body temperature rose, they undressed slowly. Yet, failure to warm them quickly would cause the body core temperature to drop even further, resulting in phenomena and death.

Once thawed out, to stop their un-controllable shivering, they were rubbed with oil and once dressed in warm pyjamas were popped into bed with another warm body (preferably female) they are warmer and smell sweeter! This practice is known as a buddy system, which along with a warm non-alcoholic drink helps to raise and maintain the body temperature as well as raise the core temperature caused by protracted immersion in such cold water.

"With the men now safely back on board, the dory was simply left to the mercy of the sea for being so small, with a bit of luck it would most probably be washed ashore during the night. With the vessel now firmly attached to the buoy, the engine and drive line to the propeller were neutralised and the vessel under the influence of the onshore breeze from the west blowing east across the isthmus, slowly swung about and facing its bow towards the island. Taking up the strain on the hawser, the Polly Woodside came to rest and rode easily on the anchorage. The diesel engine was shut down and the vessel closed up for the evening. With the exception of those cuddled up in bed drinking warm soup and thawing out, the entire ship's compliment sat down to a well-earned dinner.

"The crew were justly proud of their achievement, for as pure novices they had with the most primitive of navigational equipment, a sexton and a gimbal compass combined with a set of very old maritime maps of the southern latitudes, achieved their goal. As a totally inexperienced crew with a sailing vessel almost two centuries old and a bare hand full of people that knew anything about it, they had successfully challenged the worst seas in the world. The roaring forties and the furious fifties and defying all the odds had safely reached their destination. The meal over, it was all hands to the dishes, clean up the galley and put everything away.

"Here in this lonely, hostile, windswept southern region, unpredictable and violent winds can come away from a different quarter or change directions suddenly and without warning. Therefore, for safety sake, a night watchman and a lookout was posted. One to watch the weather and one to watch the other. For without a timely warning of a sudden change in the weather pattern, they too would simply become another statistic with their vessel like so many before them, washed ashore and wrecked. In particular, one stranded on this vary beach in the December of 1987 was the MV Nella Dan, lovingly known to all who had sailed in her over a 25-year period as little red ship. She to now rests on the bottom of the sea 3000 fathoms down.

Wrecked on Macquarie Island Dec.1987. Refloated by Austpac Salvage (Drysdale) and after catching fire scuttled in 3000 fathoms 10 nautical miles east of the Nuggets

"Like Miles Holding, first officer of the 'Perseverance', the first recorded vessel to have discovered this island on the 10th of July 1810. Ivan, standing on the stern fantail, studied the long, dark outline of the island and his thoughts turned to the distant past when in 1810, the brigantine rigged sealing vessel 'The Perseverance', had hove too at this very spot and Miles, as the first officer called throughout the night through his megaphone. Ahoy there ashore, this is the good ship 'Perseverance' out of Sydney cove and bound for the same. Is there anyone ashore,' as he looked with some apprehension at the darkened foreshore of this virgin island.

"However, call as he may, no answer was forthcoming, nor was there the flickering twinkle of an oil lamp to be seen anywhere along the darkened foreshore. That day, they had accidentally discovered an uninhabited island. Tonight however, as Ivan knew it was in fact deserted again, there was no need to call the island seeking inhabitants.

"Ivan as a younger man, when the officer in charge of two separate Australian National Antarctic Research Expeditions to this very island well over half a century ago. He had also hove to twice at this very spot in the icebreaker 'MV Nella Dan'. The vessel mentioned, which now lies in 3000 fathoms of water some ten nautical miles east of the Nuggets, just a short distance from where they now lay at anchor. During that period, he had wintered for two long years and had experienced not only the loneliness and heartbreak of its total isolation; but also, the fury of the elements and the despair of experiencing the cold semi-darkness of the Sub-Antarctic winters that he knew so well.

Tonight, as though it was only yesterday, the same evening sky was once more lit by majestic colourful 'southern auroras', which raced back and forth across the dark southern sky. He remembered only too well; the Southern Cross and the million stars that tonight shone down on him once more as close and as bright as they did all those years ago. While far to the south, the incredible coloured curtains of fire once more hung momentarily where they were left suspended by the brilliant ever moving auroras that lit up the horizon in the dark cloudless sky above the Antarctic Continent; alternatively, racing back and forth, as they played across the lonely southern skies. It was a celestial scene; no artist's brush could capture.

"As someone cuddle up against him seeking shelter out of the cold evening wind and asked him a question, he did not have to look to see who it was, he knew.

"'Have you really missed it all that much, or are you worried what tomorrow will bring?' Margaret said a she too looked with fascination at the distant, ever-moving, colourful horizon.

"'No, Margaret,' he replied, placing a warm comforting arm about her shoulder, 'I was really thinking 'beyond tomorrow' and all the other tomorrows that will follow. It looks as though I'm the officer in charge again and somehow that responsibility worries me more this time. "Am I capable of guiding this diverse group of very old and very young people along the right path?

"'It is going to be difficult with every one living in each other's pocket for the first time in their lives, and I might add; in harmony.'

"'God only knows how long we will be here, for some of us like you and I, it will be forever…are you sorry that you came?'

"'No, of course I am not sorry!' And hastened to add, 'I was all those years ago when you left me behind on so many of your southern voyages.'

"'But no,' Margaret volunteered, 'you just wait and see my lad, we will cope.'

"'What was it you used to say?' She laughed trying to remember an expression she had heard many times so long ago.

"'Oh yes, once an ANARE bod always an ANARE bod.'

Placing an arm around his waist urging him towards the focsle, 'Come onto bed fearless leader,' she laughed, 'we have a lot to do tomorrow.'"

Chapter 12
A New Beginning

"The following morning, the three deep-sea swimmers or the newly inducted members of the elite * 'Antarctic Blue Balls Club' were with no apparent after effects up and about. Incredibly, for this time of the year, the morning sun shone bright and warm on the small group of people already clustered on deck most of whom because of the perpetual rain in their former homeland had never seen a sunrise. However, on this first incredible day of a new way of life, there was not a cloud in the sky and better still not a drop of rain. It was a glorious day to be alive.

"Down below in the cold, grey waters, thousands of gentoo, rock hopper, royal and king penguins, porpused quickly past the vessel towards the shoreline. Many hundreds of fur seals played and frolicked around the ship. While occasionally and to the delight the younger generation, elephant seals of immense proportions surfaced close to the vessel like miniature submarines blowing water and air bubbles high in the air from their large inflated trunk like proboscis or nose.

"Above the vessel and in fact along the entire length of the island, many thousands of sea birds of varying sizes and species filled the sky in a dazzling display of paired or lone flights. They hovered on the onshore winds or above the waves crashing ashore along the eastern cliff, face away to the south or sweeping down occasionally between the troughs as they searched for food amongst the waves that pounded inshore hour after hour. While others riding the air currents played or hovered on the wind shear above the high cliff tops; macronette's hali or giant petrels in their quest for food, winged silently past on their never-ending beach patrol.

"The previous evening, it had been agreed that Tim and a crew would stay and look after the vessel while Ivan, Peter, Adrian and Matthew a former merchant navy engineer would go ashore in a long boat and check out the station. In hindsight, what would they have given for the dear old LARC now!

"A ship's long boat was hoisted from its davits and lowered over the side, once settled on the rising-falling swell that swept continually past the vessel on its never-ending race towards the shore. The four intrepidies clambered down the Jacob's ladder and dropped safely into it, once the lines were cast off, Ivan took the tiller and his three companions pulled for the shore. Pulling into Buckles Bay they rode a breaking wave in through one of the rocky chutes right up to the rough shingled beach. Leaping out, they dragged the long boat high up into the tussock grass beyond the reach of the incoming wash where it would be safe from the advancing and receding waves.

"As anticipated and showing only a few superficial scratches, the small dory was discovered washed up amongst the rocks. God only knows where the oars were, but they will eventually turn up. Taking time out to right the little painter, they carried it further up the beach into the tussocks, and deposited it away from the incoming waves. After all those months at sea, as everyone stood there involuntarily swaying back and forth for some time, it took quite a while to regaining their equilibrium. What a strange feeling it was to stand once more on firm, stable ground that was neither rolling, lifting nor falling away. Finally, when everyone was steady on their feet, they marched in single file along the edge of the water, following a parade of colourful king penguins fully intent on doing the same.

"Covering most, if not all, of the open spaces where many hundreds of small yearling elephant seals that lay shoulder to shoulder. In some places, they were so closely packed together, that the men simply ran across their backs, making the journey up to the living quarters a most exciting and interesting experience to say the least.

"Once up on the old original road, which runs from the living quarters down the sandy isthmus on the eastern side of the station, along the front of the buildings in the work area and extending up to the remote radio transmitters at the southern end of the isthmus, they came to the workshop area. With some degree of difficulty, the foursome, fighting the rusty creaking door hinges on the garage door; managed to open it enough to peer inside. Inside the building and to their delight protected by plastic cocoons were a small tractor with a 500-gallon tanker on a flatbed trailer behind it. A large quad drive D10-Caterpillar trax-cavator with a bucket and a blade on the front of it and believe it or not a LARC like amphibian and finally a small hover craft, both of which sitting on safety stands clear of the floor.

"Next door, the old hydrogen-generating shed for the metrological section, seemed to have changed little. Then the Met office complete with radio sonde-room and balloon release shed, stood locked and secure. Secure yes, but since green laser met beams took over from balloon flights many years ago, this building is not used any more. Behind this row of buildings and in the centre of the isthmus, the large-brick scientific and administration building situated high above the surrounding stagnant pools of seal wallows and tussock grass; still stood safe and secure. As he and his men of the 32nd ANARE had completed this building during his last year on the island, Ivan remembered this large building well and had no need to look in there.

"Back on the road on the eastern side of the station, the last building, again all closed up, was the radio shack. A peep in the salt-stained window showed the contents to be secure and intact under plastic covers, it looked as if everything had been in working order when closed up. Down across the long, sandy isthmus they walked. This area normally a temporary home too and covered with hundreds of sleeping, moulting juvenile elephant seals, was completely deserted. However, because the winter had already set in, Ivan re-called that in his time there would not normally been any here anyway. Also, a strange, flat odour that he could not identify lay heavily on the westerly wind and an eerie silence permeated the area. Something was definitely out of character here, but for the life of him; he could not see what it was.

"Arriving at the living quarters, and climbing up over the sturdy rock security fence that surrounded the living quarters, which included the main powerhouse, hospital, living quarters, water storage tanks and numerous bulk stores.

Normally a structure like this fence would have been rubbed smooth by itching, scratching elephant seals during the moulting season, but strangely enough, it was covered with lichens and moss; It would appear that no seal had lain up against it or rubbed the hair off itself against this protective barrier in many years. Why?

"One by one, they checked out the buildings, which after many decades of being closed up were cold, damp and musty. However once opened and aired they would prove to be quite serviceable. When the engines in the powerhouse were checked and started and the power restored to the station, with little or no effort the large station would not only be liveable, but also quite comfortably.

"The large, round concrete water tanks built into the side of small hillock on the eastern side of the living quarters were full and overflowing. It would seem that the poly piping up to the little dam at the top of Gadgets Gully some three miles southeast of the station; was still intact.

"The last and most important thing was to get the Polly Woodside in off the open sea. To do this they were required to build a small lagoon and the best place for this was in front of the area called Boat Harbour, a landing place once used by the original sealers almost three centuries ago. This small area was between the small hillock where the water tanks stood and Smugglers cove at the south-eastern base of North Head, which rose steeply from the water's edge at this point. Here a series of deep, rocky chutes ran out into the sea behind a large rocky offshore promontory and once cleared of rocks and kelp, the vessel could be safely towed in through this chute into the proposed lagoon. Therefore, the conditions in boat harbour were important.

"Climbing over the back fence they walked down to the edge of the sea and looked at the small kelp filled shute. On checking the area, it was agreed that by using the large Caterpillar front-end loader, with little trouble the kelp in the landing area could be cleared out into deep water. Then within the living compound, a small lagoon could be dug in front of the chute, and using both the engines of the vessel and the small amphibian, the vessel could be brought in off the high seas and secured out of the elements. Happy with what they had seen, they now turned their attention to the immediate problems, the first of which was to get the power restored and once this was achieved everything else would quickly fall into place.

"Climbing back over the fence, the small group pushed their way through the thick, waist-high tussock grass, which had overgrown the narrow boardwalks within the living complex and made their way back to the powerhouse. Once inside, they removed the plastic cocoons from the three large Caterpillar engines, cooling towers, alternators and exciters and finally power consoles. They drained the inhibitor from the sump of the engines, replaced the oil filters and refilled the engines with fresh lubricating oil. Once started, these particular engines would run straight up to full revs before the governors cut in, therefore after standing for God knows how many years, to manually prime the oil pressure system they had to be barred over many times. This is done to stop the initial lack of oil pressure damaging the crankshaft bearings, valve train, piston rings and turbo charger bearings, before oil pressure was built up.

"From amongst the many cases stored along the wall of the storeroom, they located a set of brand new 12-volt batteries, which they filled with a 1275 spec/gravity electrolyte (a sulphuric acid mix), which was stored in large crated earthenware demijohns. Once filled, the batteries were placed in their racks on the engine. A portable motor-driven Honda battery charger, once serviced and started, was connected to them to top up the charge. As Ivan and Adrian, were both mechanical engineers, bringing the engines into service held no fears, in fact it was right up their alley.

"While the batteries were being charged, all the buildings within the living area were opened and the power switches or main distribution circuit breaker were switched off, the last thing they needed was a short circuit and a fire in an unoccupied building. The mess or dining room was opened; then the large bulk refrigerators and bulk food stores were opened and checked for contents.

"Having checked the entire base and made sure that every power circuit was turned off, Ivan and Adrian returned to the powerhouse. After draining off a quantity of stale fuel, they hand-primed and bled the injection systems and finally connected the fully charged batteries they set about starting the engines. If the engines had been serviceable when they were shut down, they should start without any problem.

"'You right, Mitta Moody,' Ivan said to his long-time friend as he studied the all too familiar control panel.

"'Yep, as right as we ever will be, I suppose,' Adrian replied nonchalantly, 'come on, press the bloody button!'

"The resounding *"clack"* of the starter solenoid being energised in that long silent powerhouse sounded so loud and distinct, the silence of the powerhouse closed for many decades was shattered by the sudden impatient high-pitched whirring of the starter motor as it spun the huge engine faster and faster. Gaining compression, the engine fired and missed, fired and missed several times, then all of a sudden roared into life and up went the rpms.

"Slowly, the great turbo charger started to spin, faster and faster, until finally the high-pitched whine of the blowers spinning at 32 thousand rpms pushing 1·2 inches Hg of thrust, the dull, thumping roar of the large engine echoed once more out across the long silent, deserted station.

"As they watched, the wavering needles on the voltage metre slowly but surely climbed upwards, 100, 150, 200, 215, 240 volts. The needle on the cycle meter swung lazily back and forth, as the engine steadily gained temperature and the blowers settled down to a constant speed. Over riding the governor with a manual throttle over-ride, Ivan settled the revs down to a steady 50 cycles. With one engine now going, the same procedure was repeated with the second and third engines, only this time without as much pressure on the operators; they too started up quickly and settled down to run smoothly.

"After so many years of inactivity, the engines were left to warm up and normalise. Coolant was drawn off from the water pumps to make sure that no accumulated air bubbles were left in the cooling towers or heater pipes, which ran throughout the living quarters. This air would create electrolysis that would eat holes in the cylinder heads. This done, the water levels were topped up and the foursome then walked down to the beach in and out hundreds of yearling elephant seals that still crowded along the foreshore and waved to the small crowd clustered on deck. Yes, those onboard could hear the engines and now seeing their men folk by the water edge knew that everything was all right.

"Leaving one person at the work area, one in the living quarters and one in the bulk store area, Ivan returned to the powerhouse and closed the circuit breaker to the main distribution console. For the first time in many years, all along the control panel, dozens of small red, green and white display LEDs (light emitting diodes) flickered and lit up to glow in all their splendour. While some simply flickered for a little while, went *'Pop'* and burnt out, but before they did, they indicated that the circuit existed. Later when the station had settled down to a routine and a permanent staff were in charge of the powerhouse and distribution system, most probably him and a few trainees, these blown light emitting diodes, would be replaced.

"With the second engine synchronised, it too was and brought online and the non-existent load shared between them at 240 Volts x 50 cycles while the third engine, now known to be serviceable and not being required at the moment, was shut down. Then one by one the circuit breakers to the various buildings and workshops were closed, (switched on) and as the load was taken up, both engines would share it. Finally, with the entire station online, the automatic load-sharing device would balance out the load evenly between both engines from that point on. Closing the door to the powerhouse, Ivan proceeded to check all the buildings with each member checking that area. At the refrigerated cool room, which was initially left closed, the refrigerant compressors were turned on. Down across the isthmus, although a few safety lights were blown and some street lighting was missing, a few bulbs here and there, electrically the station appeared quite serviceable.

Returning to the garage on the isthmus, with very little trouble the diesel-powered amphibian was started and with power now available throughout the station, the air compressor was checked and simply switched on and left to build up pressure. Then the large all-terrain tyres on the amphibian were inflated and with the aid of a trolley jack, the vehicle was lifted from its safety stands, and lowered to the ground. After a quick squirt of oil on the hinges, with some degree of effort and against much opposition from the dozens of sleeping juvenile elephant seals leaning against the doors, which should have long since gone to sea, but still lay on the road outside the door, the doors of the garage were pushed reluctantly open. Making a mental note that when we had settled down, the first thing to do was to get the younger generation to clean and oil all the door hinges before they broke.

"Searching through the draws of the filing cabinet, they found the operator's manual for the mini-amphibian and set about learning how to make it move. As the controls were relatively simple, once moving it was driven a few laps up and down the narrow road in front of the work area. Again, only after many indignant elephant seal pups were enticed to move back off what was once the road. This was achieved by various means, blowing the horn, revving up the engine and the odd, gentle nudge in the bum with the front of the mini-LARC!

"As the sun started to sink on the western side of the island, as it was pointless leaving some one ashore simply to keep an eye on the powerhouse, the circuit breakers were opened and before being shut down for the night, the engines were idled down and allowed to cool. Once everything was closed up, the foursome climbed up on the mini-LARC and with the long boat in tow, motored back out to the 'Polly Woodside' which was now riding easily on the anchorage. Leaving the LARC tied off on two strong hawsers astern of the vessel, the long boat was winched back on board and secured on its davits once more.

"After dinner that evening, a group discussion decided that while the weather held, tomorrow they would take everyone ashore in the Mini LARC while at the same time towing the long boat loaded with stores behind it. Landing them on the beach, boatload after boatload until everyone, with the exception of a skeleton crew, which would remain on board, were ashore. It was the task of those taken ashore to get the station up and running ASAP. While this was going on, a crew would stay on the LARC and continue unloading the stores dropping everything in the main Bulk store. When everything was safely ashore and under cover, the sorting and packing things away would commence as soon as the station was up and running and things had settled down.

"In crisp mid-winter weather amongst the first group to go ashore the following morning were Ivan and Mitta Moody, their task was to re-start the main engines and turn on the power and lighting. This done, they switched on the refrigerators and cool stores compressors, which they had checked yesterday. Light the oil stove in the mess and once the water in the engine cooling towers was up to temperature, turn on the heaters to the living quarters letting the hot water from the engines circulate throughout the station to help dry them out.

"They would then start up the large tracked front-end loader and after a quick introduction as to how a trax-cavator worked; indoctrinate several willing helpers in how to operate it, also how and where to construct the small lagoon. However, they first had to clear an opening down through the tussocks and the seal fence to allow the LARC up into the living quarters and the stores area. That done, commence digging the chute out into deep water into boat harbour to bring the Polly Woodside in, eventually pulling her up into the small man-made lagoon. Once the vessel was up away from the ravages of the sea, the lagoon would be sealed off and the protective rock fence replaced across the beach area. As one day, a future generation would need her to return to civilisation, a group discussion convened after the rock wall adjacent to muggler's cove was rebuilt, decided that once the vessel was secured against the inner wall of the lagoon, it would be stripped of all fittings right down to deck level and covered with a plastic cocoon."

* An elite club for those members have swum naked in Antarctic waters at mid-winter.

Chapter 13
Organisation – For The Want Of A Name

"While this freak, but unusually good winter weather continued, they had to get a station of this size up and running in a very short period of time. All the stores and equipment from the ship had to be un-loaded, un-packed and stacked away in the large bulk store, with the perishables, such as meat and fish and other perishables to go into the refrigerators. The new women's quarters built during the late 1900s and situated under North Head would become home to the married couples. The Southern Aurora or the main 18-room living quarters on the eastern side of the living quarters would be home to the females. While the large 16-room donga or living quarters located on the northeastern end of the living quarters in front of boat harbour, would be home to the single men and boys.

"The Station Hospital dedicated to Dr Robert Millard for his skill and expertise in prolonging the life of our summer biologist, Roger Barker so many years ago (1979) appropriately named 'Millard' was re-opened; Robert Millard had been a young expedition locum from Ceres, a small farming community situated in the Barrabool Hills south west of the City of Geelong in Victoria, Australia. Robert, by his skill and devotion attending one of the early expedition members, critically injured in a fall so many years before, had won the hearts and respect of all ANARE members on the island at that time.

"Now the new Doc, with the aid of two of the female cadets who were training as nurses, commenced to check its contents and restock it with the latest drugs and robotic operating equipment we had brought with us…so that area was now covered. The large bulk food store was re-opened and from it, enough dry rations were carried across the compound in time to get the first evening meal under way and to re-stock the mess and the dining room complex.

"As scones (biscuits) and damper for today had been baked on board ship, the previous evening, to make fresh bread for tomorrow, dry yeast powder was mixed with warm water and put up on a rack in the warmth above the stove to brew. Crockery and cutlery was washed and the large mess hall swept and dusted along with the hundreds of 45&78 RPM records, video tapes, CDs and DVDs, which were stacked around the walls of the dining room come recreation room and finally the many tables there were set. From the clothing store, new linen, blankets and towels were issued; these were aired and placed on every bed for the occupants now moving in, as well as those still working outside on other various chores.

"So, by the end of that first hectic day, the station as though it had never been closed, was running smoothly. Finally, the livestock was brought ashore and corralled for the time being inside the living area along the steep southern wall of North Head, while the assorted poultry were temporarily housed in the old sealers chapel. Later, using wire netting that was once used to fence off specific areas safe from rabbit predation, a suitable weatherproof roost or chicken coop would be erected and they would all be moved outside. Also, once livestock corrals had been built, the animals would be moved to Red River and permanently ranged within that protected valley before final allocation in the coming spring to the various out stations around the island.

"That first evening combined with the mournful wail of the evening westerly breeze as it sprung up from the west, the pleasant relaxing sounds of canned music, the click of pool balls striking one another and the genuine infectious laughter of the younger group, the once silent deserted station seemed so alive. Slowly, as the lights were extinguished one by one, this unique satellite community settled down for what was to be a lifetime of such nights in this their new home, Macquarie Island.

"In the days that followed, there did not seem to be enough hours in the day as people attended to their new allotted tasks. Duty rosters were made up, a slushy roster (Mess assistant) to help the older women assigned to control the cooking. A list of messing responsibilities was drawn up and powerhouse training had also commenced. While on the social side, as he was good at making home brew, Wayne while the ingredients lasted would be chief brewing officer responsible for making the beer. This was as well as his many other duties, such as electrician, a community radio station and communications training, all a very important side of life in such a confined isolated co-existence to make life run as normally and smoothly as possible were established.

"By the end of the third day, the kelp in the small chute which rose up out of the sea in boat harbour had been cleared out into deep water, the small lagoon had been excavated and readied for flooding deep enough to float the Polly Woodside inshore. Once the dividing wall was removed between the sea and the lagoon flooded, the vessel would to be floated into the living area, where she would be safe from the ravages of the sea, also to keep hull her wet and stopping her from drying out and becoming a tad rusty.

"When all this groundwork had been completed, the exacting task of bringing the Polly Woodside in off the high sea was attempted. Unfortunately, a freshening south-easterly swell proved too great and the vessel was only saved from destruction by skill of the coxswain and the vessels powerful auxiliary engine. Finally, at 3 Am on the fourth morning, the sea was down as flat as a millpond and the duty watch hurriedly woke the crewmembers.

"Everyone involved in the docking of the vessel were quickly roused and once dressed set off down to the chute in boat harbour where the mini-LARC was driven into the sea to stand off the end of the reef and take the vessel in tow. Once under way, the vessel was brought into the trough, where pushed by its own powerful auxiliary engine…pulled and guided at the bow by the little mini-LARC, it was brought safely up through the chute and across the channel in the pebbled beach area. Here the cable from the mini-LARC was transferred to the larger and more powerful Quad D10 tractor. Now attached to the vessel by the strong steel cable, it proceeded to pull the 'Polly Woodside' into the small lagoon. Once up against the internal wall of the lagoon, several hawsers attached to the stern and bow, secured the 'Polly

Woodside' bow first into the prevailing westerly wind, there cushioned by several large rubber tyres, she was securely braced in the upright position.

"The entrance to the lagoon was now sealed off, the security fence rebuilt and over the next few weeks, the vessel would be stripped of everything required later to make her seaworthy once more. The yard arms, riggings, ropes and finally masts would all be dismantled, removed and along with the sails once dry, would be stored away in the large bulk store until required. Finally, the exposed hull would be covered in a plastic cocoon to keep out of the elements.

"Those first few days passed by so quickly and so fast that no one had time to think about anything except getting the job done; well except when it was time for lunch or dinner. As meal times drew near, it did not take long for the mouth-watering aroma of freshly baked bread or the tantalizing aroma of food wafting from the direction of the mess to arouse the pangs of hunger. After dinner on the first Saturday night ashore, a round table conference was held to decide on and to set the following rules; rules for their continued survival, which would be adopted and adhered too. The leader of this small group would be Ivan, assisted by the three oldest men and women as a committee. As leader, he was also responsible for rationing all amenities, including the beer and wine ration scale according to what supplies they had and to oversee the day-to-day activities, station running as well as arbitrating on local disagreements.

"Robbin the doctor and Jake the Padre would be responsible for the health, diet and the mental well-being of every one with medical training and mid-wifery clinics started, so that in the event of anything happening to him, there would always be doctors and nurses available to take over.

"Wayne would be responsible for all communications and radio instruction and with an assistant, the master brewer or beer maker, and all beer-making sessions would be a community affair.

"Peter the ex-naval commander, training division, would be training officer and commence schools in all phases of education, science and mechanics. While Ivan and Mitta Moody would run the automotive, mechanical and engineering trade school, where apprentices would be inducted, these would include shift operators for the powerhouse and power distribution systems. The older women, each of whom had a special forte, would cater for the specific needs of the younger females who would become involved in cooking, confectionery manufacture, bread making and sewing and dressmaking skills.

"'Alvario,' Lisa's dad, a master cabinet maker and carpenter would be responsible for carpentry apprentices and would also be responsible for the maintenance of all buildings and repairs to the station as well as the upgrade of all the out stations later. All scientific studies and observations would recommence where people were able to do so.

"Lisa was elected scribe and public notary and her job was to be that of an official clerk, listing the history and whereabouts of the islands inhabitants from this point on… Names, families, marriages, births and when the day came… deaths.

"Movies selected from the vast collection of stored film, CD Rom and DVDs would be screened once a week on Saturday evenings. All birthdays, wedding anniversaries, mid-winter and festive dinners would be best dress; with clean casual dress every other evening. Finally, the stock would be moved to Red River and initially watched over by the two females brought along for that purpose; however, as they had now integrated so well into the community, it was hard to tell who was who.

"It was quite obvious from the onset, that the group was too large for the station to run smoothly, well that is without some one-stepping on some toes. So, it was decided to open up the outlying sub-stations and set up young family groups with an older couple as a steadying influence at each of them, thereby distributing the group impact evenly on the community as well as the environment. It was also quite obvious that when boy meets girl, and as they were living under one another's feet day in and day out, that some were prone to become inseparable, insensible, infatuated and finally impregnated! So, to this end, Padre Jake conducted family planning nights and open sex discussions with the doctors became part of the weekly routine. For until the group eventually dispersed to other out stations and the youngsters were married, no un-wanted children for a new generation were scheduled.

"In a normal co-existence this sort situation would never arise, but here we have a group of healthy, incredibly fit young people that would never live a normal suburban life, nor experience any of the mechanical pleasures of life. There were no pub nights, no pre-dawn discos, and no rave parties. They also had the added responsibility to be the fathers and mothers of a new generation of people that will walk this island and maybe this earth long after we have gone, thrust upon them, so it was important that they get the best start possible.

"Once schooling and trade training was finished, those of a sensible age, realising their role in this unique community and had picked their future partners, would be married in the quaint little wooden 'Sealers Chapel', which has stood here on the western side of the living quarters for more than two and a half centuries. Well, that was after we got the chooks out of there!

"Throughout the remaining winter period, those moving out in the coming spring would make and prepare their own equipment and select which other couples they would like to live with, and in which area. Once these groups were established and the weather permitting, the little amphibian would to put to sea and those out stations would be checked. Restocking, modifying and upgrading would be carried out so that by the middle of the coming spring those migrating further south or west to Caroline Cove, would all be settled in their upgraded future homes. There, they would elect their own leader responsible to the main group and set out their own programs for existence.

"As communications on 5.4 MHz to all the outlying station worked well, a regular evening communications network would be introduced. No one, travelling or living around the island, would be cut off for any protracted period. Besides, in case of an injury or birth, in good weather conditions and using the Mini-LARC, it was only a short trip back to the hospital at the main station. If not, it was only a day's walk to or from the most distant living quarters.

"While all this feverish departure activity was going on, Ivan took time out to check out the area around north head for signs of any wreckage as well as inspecting both sides of the isthmus during which time he came upon an incredible sight on the western side of the isthmus. There were dried out seal carcasses everywhere! It would appear that the large elephant seal harem, which was annually located here on the centre/western side of the isthmus called Camp Beach, had all perished since coming ashore.

"What could have caused the death of so many hundreds of seals? Dehydrated carcasses of the large aggressive beach masters, hundreds of cows and pups littered the area. This was certainly the cause of unusual stench that he had smelt when they first came ashore. Also, this could be the reason that no seals were evident on the centre of the isthmus.

"But why?

"It was also quite obvious to an old hand that the hundreds of gentoo penguins, which for centuries had normally fussed about the isthmus and nested on or under the trampled down tussock grass in this immediate area even in winter, were no longer evident. There were a few small colonies further down the isthmus towards the razor back ridge at the southern end, but certainly, nothing like there once used to be.

"In the centre of the isthmus between the cenotaph, Radio shack and the new science building, there was and always had been a large seal wallow, but today it seemed much bigger than he recalled. Muddy slide marks here and there down the walls of it and the odd air bubble coming to the surface to eventually explode in a shower of muddy fragments certainly seemed to indicate that there were seals in it, yet strangely, there were no seals obvious in this area.

"Here the smell of death and decay was almost over powering, an uneasy feeling about all this made him move back away from the edge; it was as though from down there in the depths of that quagmire, someone or something was watching him!

"However, what or who could be watching him, nothing human could live down there in that cesspool of mud, excrement and urine… or was it human?

"Backing away from the wallow, he made his way back up to the hospital and asked the Doc to get him a sample of the gas coming from the wallow and determine what it could be.

"'Oh, and by the way,' he added, 'keep back from the edge, I don't want you or any one going near it until we find out what is going on.'

Chapter 14
So Much to Do And So Little Time

"Soon after arrival, Doc and Wayne had set up a fish hatchery and breeding tanks in the old IPSO/UAP (Upper Atmosphere Physics) building and introduced the thousands of hatchlings, crustaceans and eggs they had brought. Therefore, by the end of the coming spring they would be ready to introduce them into the many selected, protected lakes. The larger surviving fingerlings had been fed and immediately introduced into the large protected lakes at Green Gorge, Waterfall Lake and Red River where they would be fed on a weekly basis with the pelletized food they were used too and, which had been brought specifically for that purpose.

"To up-grade the station working 'Bees' were established. With paths linking the living quarters and the central compound between the buildings over grown with tussock grass cleared. To the older teenagers and therefore the fittest, went the job of enlarging the small fresh water catchment or dam, which was situated up on the edge of the Plateau above the eastern side of the island at the head of 'Gadgets Gully'. In its present form, this small dam would not provide the volume of water required to support the sudden increase in population. For those teenagers, this daily excursion up onto the plateau, the challenge of climbing the steep mountainside 1000 feet up Gadgets Gully Day after day, drew them closer together and reinforcing the bonds already created on the voyage down.

"They were happy carefree days and the death of their friends during the epic voyage slipped further and further from their mind, as hand in hand they helped one another up the incredibly steep rocky base of 'Gadgets Gully'. Climbing the rickety old rusty steel ladders from one level to another while dragging behind them poly piping miles of poly pipe, new timbers and thick planks required to construct a larger dam and a stronger, higher retaining wall. They helped one another to ferry shovels, heavy backpacks containing tools, poly sealant and fittings. By the time, the new dam was completed and the cool clear water gurgled merrily through the strainer into the new poly pipe to commence its mad headlong rush down the mountainside the few miles along the Isthmus and up into the storage tanks. Many of the young couples engaged in this project had teamed up for life. Before the winter had elapsed, engagement parties and marriages would set the seal on their future.

"Meanwhile down in the workshops, a new skirt had been fitted to the Hovercraft and after servicing the engine, it was started and the vehicle test driven out in the calm waters of Hassle borough Bay to the west of the isthmus. This way, if the vessel malfunctioned, it would be blown ashore, where as if it were to the east in Buckles Bay it would be blown all the way to South America. To the un-educated standing on the beach watching, it may have looked as though the operators were really having a lot of fun out there, but that was not the case. The little craft seemed to have a mind of its own, the controls and the force of the blower certainly taking some time to get used too; eventually comfortable in the knowledge that they could now manoeuvre it safely; it was brought safely ashore and housed once more.

"Away back in the 19th century about 1857, there was an introduced fowl on the island called a 'Weka'. This bird was brought to the island as a source of food by the early sealers from a place called Ruggedy on Stewart Island south of New Zealand. Naturally, some escaped from vessels wrecked along the eastern foreshore, and over the next 100 years, they survived to inhabit most reaches of the island. However, in 1988-1989 in the name of science, this small reddish-brown bird about the size of a bantam fowl had supposedly been eradicated.

"Why? Supposedly it was not indigenous to the island.

"Yet, as luck would have it, Mother Nature made sure that not all had been wiped out and today, the Weka breeding undisturbed for the last one and a half centuries, was quite common once more. The younger generation were given the task of trapping or netting as many weeks as possible and setting them up in pens with ample natural grass cover to domesticate them for eggs and later for use as table birds.

"In the coming spring, this same group of chicken wranglers would be responsible for collecting one out of every two freshly lain Royal penguin eggs from the nearby rookeries at Sandy Bay. These would be washed, stacked in egg crates, which would be turned every week to stop the yolks settling to the bottom of the shell and breathing, consequently going bad or alternatively preserve them between layers of wet seaweed in the cool store. This would look after egg situation for each coming year and ensure an additional food source, as well as a main ingredient for cakes and biscuits.

"With the food situation seemingly well in hand, while they had fresh meat now, as well as the nucleus of a breeding program with the red deer, goats and sheep, as well poultry. As it would be several years before the stock had multiplied enough to start killing in the mean time they could live on seal meat and royal penguins. The only problem that could arise over the next few years would be a shortage of fossil fuel to generate power. Although solar panels already installed, generated enough power to look after the station and the scientific equipment during the spring and summer, during the long dark months of winter the station would need an alternative source of power. A stock take of the plant and equipment available on the station revealed that there were enough spares to make a large wind generator.

"One of several spare 240V A/C alternators held in storage could be mounted on top of a windmill, a turntable, with slip rings connected to spring loaded carbon-bronze brushes on the bottom fixed plates. These in turn would conduct the current down a four-wire copper covered pyrotenic cable to the powerhouse. Alternatively, if normal rubber or plastic-coated cable were to be used, the local mouse population would happily dine on it and short circuit the whole system. Any one of several spare hovercraft propellers, which were located in the garage, apparently used over the years and removed when theoretically time expired, could power this.

"This cable would terminate on the three phase buzz bars in the distribution console at the powerhouse, when not in use or during the blizzard season the blades to stop them self-destructing, would be feathered out of the wind and it would cease to spin. With the constant westerly winds screaming over North Head and the station, this electrical generation system would support the station indefinitely thereby saving their critical reserves of fossil fuel. It was necessary to manufacture a windmill style tower, the turntable and fan mounting, a coupling and put it all together up on the small grassy knoll behind the powerhouse or on western edge of north head where there was definitely no shortage of wind. As all the out stations were already equipped with medium size wind generators and a battery storage system, supplemented by solar power cells, which were ample during the day light hours of spring and summer, there would be ample power for the inhabitants for the time being.

"If the proposed wind generator proved successful, a second one would be built and set up on the southern end of the island. This would provide ample power for the Caroline Cove and Hurd Point Settlements. It would then seem that all contingencies to assure a stable existence had been covered. This first year, everyone would work towards the build-up of stores, rebuilding and the modification of all the out-stations. Except when the seas were not calm, which was most infrequent here, the new inhabitants, acting as porters, would carry all stores and equipment overland.

"Those who were destined to take up residence in a particular out-station during the coming spring would naturally concentrate on that area. Where people had a preference, the future sites were allotted accordingly.

However, where there were two or more seeking the same area, lots were drawn and every one was to abide by that final decision. The final allocated areas and inhabitants were:

Dean and Lisa, their immediate family and one couple to Sandy Bay. Here they would control most of the stock for this end of the island in the broad valley above and to the right of the brother's track.

Dave and Emma, Dominic and Teelah, one of the former Feral girls would look after the stock and the fish program in the Red River area, here, where most of the red deer and goats would also be free ranged and bred.

The MacFarlane family and one couple, Angie the other Feral girl and Aub, one of the cadets, would manage the Green Gorge area. As it was central to all out stations, this would be the central works for processing fresh deer, goat and seal meat and the tanning of selected animal and seal hides, which would be used in the production of foot wear and heavy outer clothing. Also, build up an oil digester from one or more of the old sealers Tri pots, some of which were located on the historical cenotaph in the middle of the isthmus. The blubber from the seals would be refine and used to make oil which was essential in the production of soap, perfumes, body oils and if required in an emergency for heating and lighting. In addition, as insect life and water born larvae to support the fish, were limited, the seal meat remaining after the blubber was removed, could be used to make palletised food for the fish farms. From here, the inhabitants would also monitor the fish introduced into the large lake situated in the base of the hidden valley beyond the eastern walls of the island, and immediately behind the living quarters.

"Additional work for Barry and his party, was the erection of stone stockyards, a slaughterhouse, and to keep the meat cool construction of a small cool room. This room built of stone and sealed with an insulation of mud, moss and seaweed covering, would have a false floor under which tons of hard packed snow and ice collected from the nearby mountain tops during the winter, would be packed. Later, a drying room and a smokehouse were proposed. It should be possible during the summer to collect, dry and store enough kelp to fire a smokehouse. In addition, they would harvest the great fields of dry Tussock grass in that area; compress it into blocks about the size of a normal house brick as an additional source of fuel. This would enable them to preserve by smoking, various meats, notably game, poultry and seal meat thereby creating an additional source of food to sustain the colony for long periods or until the wild life returned each spring.

"Peter, Sharyn and family along with one couple, Melissa and Gareth and their two children would live at and monitor the Lusitania Bay area. That area is home to the largest king penguin rookery in the world. Being open to the easterly elements it is not conducive to breeding or farming stock, so their task will be to monitor the King colony as well as assisting with the fish-breeding program a few miles north at Green Gorge.

"Set in a majestic breath taking, yet isolated spot is the living quarters of Hurd Point, which nestles precariously under the mountains on the extreme southeaster end the island. Wayne, Deidre and family and one young couple would control Hurd Point, where apart from maintaining the stock along the flat terrace under the mountains at the end of the plateau on the extreme southern end of the island. They would be responsible for monitoring the 17 hectares or 1.75 million pairs of breeding royal penguins situated there in the largest royal penguin rookery in the world. One of their tasks would be to collect the hundreds of freshly lain eggs and distribute them to the other southern settlements for the coming year. Also, on their arrival back from sea each year, whilst the penguins were plump and fat, to kill and skin up to 1000 early in the season and removing only the breast fillets for distribution as an alternative source of meat to all the other living areas. Also, convey the skins to Green Gorge to be tanned and finally delivered to the main station, where they would be converted into various size waterproof clothes and leggings.

"Wayne would be in charge of communications at the southern end of the Island which would be built on the southern terrace, work with Alan on the maintenance of the proposed wind generator. Finally, Alan and Dorthe with their family and one other couple would maintain Caroline Cove; their work here was to monitor the breeding cycle of the albatross, the wandering albatross, the black brow and the grey head. Also, the light-mantled sooty albatross. All of which inhabit the walls of Petrel Peak, Windsor Bay and the Amphitheatre south/west of Waterfall Lake. They would also be responsible for the fish program in Waterfall Lake. Build and maintain fish traps that would close off and trap any fish attempting to go over the cliff in one of the many waterfalls, where the lake discharges its over flow to cascade down the western cliff face and finally onto the tundra far below. Also, to assist Wayne with the maintenance of the wind generator."

Chapter 15
Not Just One of The Boys

"As the weeks quickly unfolded, the total effort put in by each and every one getting the station up and running; was wonderful. There were no hassles, simply an exciting new way of life with daily routines and responsibilities, responsibilities which kept each and everyone happy and fully occupied. But soon, it was quite obvious that there was something missing,

"With each passing day, the strain of living in such close confinement with one another started to tell, it was quite obvious even to the un-initiated that the station was dividing. For some, after a hard day's work, it was simply a few beers before dinner in the evening and retire to their quarters. However, for those that were married, they had the comfort of cuddling up to a warm body, satisfying their sexual demands and finally rolling over to drift off into a contented sleep. It would seem therefore, that little or if any thought had been given to the fact that this sublime island existence may not have been as full filling to other parties, as it may have been for those enjoying these creature comforts.

"In particular the younger females who were now feeling their own desires and the noticeable lack of privacy. They were quite aware of what was going on just down the hall or in the married quarters and to suppress their own desires could only clamp a cushion between their legs and squeeze hard on it; even so, it was not enough. They were not simply designated incubators, here to produce the children of tomorrow… No…they were healthy active young females who needed both physical and emotional satisfaction, the same as anyone else.

"They also needed something else; they needed to full-fill their own physical and emotional goals. Whispered conversation, not yet bordering on rebellion, but frustration… they were hell bent on creating an age-old way of life, a life that belongs only to women. They needed something that in an apparent man's world; was theirs. The whispers gained momentum and became conversation. The conversations became meetings and with all the subtly that is woman; they came up with a remedy for the situation.

"In the centre of the Isthmus, there is a large scientific block. Complete with Plant room, including engines, power supply and central heating and as well, had many large open and most of all, un-used rooms, laboratories and offices. Convening a meeting of the committee responsible for harmony within the station, a committee of women put forward their case. They wanted something that was theirs. Something strictly female and although men would be welcome from time to time, the suggestion being put forward was primarily to suit the needs of the women; needs which varied considerably to those of the men.

"For most, these things were the products of a bygone era, only a few could look after themselves and only a few could carry out feminine tasks. Skills such as knitting, spinning, yarn dyeing, needlework, tapestry, childcare, hairdressing and sowing. All the female things that belonged to them…things that gave them a purpose in life. A feeling of personal satisfaction to see a product of the own making growing steadily towards fruition. Yet for decades, modern science and robotic technology had denied them these things. Crafts and skills which over the centuries that were once handed down from mother to daughter, were now almost lost.

Here, now emancipated from the peak evolution, they were once again women who would find comfort and happiness in the simplest of things, a lace handkerchief, or a crocheted shawl. Their ability to create not only the children of tomorrow, but also the skills required to look after them; were age-old crafts that belonged to them.

"The requests were as follows.

The science block be handed over to them and set up to do the following.

One= A ladies hair dressing salon

Two= A Surgery and day clinic for future mums, with the Doctor, a Nurse and a receptionist. This would take some traffic away from the small hospital.

Three= A Beauty Salon with sauna (mixed by appointment) and massage facilities.

Four= A Day care centre.

Five= A dressmakers shop.

Six= Arts and craft manufacturing and display shop.

Seven= Photographic studio and Arts (painting) department.

Eight= Gents hairdresser. This could be combined with the hairdressing salon.

Nine = Radio Station.

"And last, but not least, a display area or a shop in the large front foyer near the OIC's office. There items they had created could be displayed or orders taken for personal items to be used in the new homes, which would soon be set up at the many out stations scattered around the island. Alternatively, if a foreign AGV or tourist craft ever arrived on the island, they would have their history on display or items, which they could barter or traded.

"Basically, the requests were simply, it was somewhere, where the women would be in their own world, talk about things that were of interest only to them and if necessary, if the isolation, the loneliness or the frustration of it all became just that little bit too much; let go and cry on someone's shoulder. Naturally, as this would certainly give added responsibility to some of the younger women and put them in an atmosphere of togetherness and learning from the older and more talented women, the idea was welcomed. With each and every one agreeing that such a complex was definitely necessary, the project was all gone and it was only Ivan who pricked up his ears at the Doc's objection.

"'Well,' he said nonchalantly, 'you will all have to be careful with any naked flames or you will blow yourself up,'

"'What do you mean by that?' Ivan asked quietly.

"'It is that seal wallow, it is giving of a very high CH_4 Methane gas reading, didn't I tell you?'

"'No, you bloody didn't,' Ivan replied angrily.

"'I recall asking you to check it and get back to me with the results but you didn't. Why the hell didn't you tell me before the women got this far, we can't stop them now or we will be forever in the poo.'

"'I don't see what all the hassle is about, the wind is always blowing east across the isthmus and out to sea, and there is no naked flame in that area,' Doc countered.

"'The hassle is, I am worried about that wallow or what is in it, it is as simple as that,' Ivan said desperately trying to keep his cool. 'I tell you this though,' he continued, 'I am going to find out what the hell is going on there, get Wayne for me.'

"'I believe you want to see me,' Wayne said casually as he approached and put down his glass of homers (beer).

"'Yes, I do, Wayne,' Ivan said, 'now listen and keep this confidential mate, there is something going on, in or around that large seal wallow on the centre of the isthmus, I want you to set up a surveillance camera and record any movement.' 'It seems,' he continued, 'that there are seals or something else moving in and out of there, however, we have never seen one on that section of the isthmus since we arrived, okay.'

"'Okay,' Wayne replied and picking up his glass of homers, held it up to the light checking the contents with a professional eye, or simply watching the rising bubbles, before turning abruptly and re-joining the crowd.

"Days and weeks flew quickly by as each and every one involved in the transformation of the scientific building set to work with a determination they did not know they possessed. Pretty handmade curtains now adorned the once bare windows and thanks to Alvario and his apprentices, new furnishing and fittings having been made, borrowed or simply scrounged from other areas suddenly appeared, also names in a bold flourish appeared on many doors indicating the new tenant.

"Finally, the older women who had the skills required to teach and instruct the younger women in all the domestic trades and skills needed, moved in and opened their doors and a whole new world of freedom was now opened to them. During the day, the large recreation room in the living quarters was now almost deserted, most of the hundreds of musical records, tapes and discs had been borrowed as 'Radio 1' Macquarie Island now boomed forth with music and local news from Radio Macca's Women's World.

"For a party to end all parties, the chance to hold a grand opening for the new community centre was too good an opportunity to miss. The first batch of the new home brew was now ready for consumption, and was put out to be chilled. Biccies and tasty home-made savouries and finger foods graced the tables, while on the veranda outside the large entrance hall, strobe lights flickered and flashed long into the night sky as the younger set danced the night away.

"All too soon, speeches were made and completed, the facility declared officially open and it was time to close up and make their way back along the Isthmus, dodging around the few sleeping elephant seals that still persisted on the island and chasing a few silly bloody Gentoo Penguins that never seem to sleep out of the way. No one seemed to notice the wind or the sleet that blew in out of the west, across Hassel borough Bay and over the Isthmus on its never-ending run around the bottom of the earth. No one ever looked out to sea, to see if there was a tell-tale light of a passing vessel or a space vehicle. No, they were at peace with their new surroundings and besides the new community centre will be open for business tomorrow.

"To prepare for the coming spring migration to the outlying station, as well as impending weddings, they had to make or learn how to make all manners of clothing and domestic Manchester, table clothes, bed linen etc. Yes, for the excited young women, tomorrow could not come soon enough.

"'Looks like we have a large seal in the living area,' someone called as they stepped over a deep muddy groove in the soft, sandy volcanic soil of the isthmus. Incredible as it seemed the muddy trail went right up too and over the wall into the living area. Once over the retaining wall and following the trail into the compound, they came upon an incredible scene; the mud trail led up to the enclosure where two nanny goats kept for milking had been housed. The fence was flattened and only the dried-out hides of the goats remained, it was as though they had been sucked out of the skins.

"'Every one inside, now, and don't come out until I say so,' Ivan shouted, ushering everyone towards the door of the mess hall.

"'Adrian, you and Pete get the heavy rifles and some ammunition out of the field store and meet me at my office, I am going to get a couple of electric stun guns.' In earlier times, these prods were sometimes used (most times) to remove large obstinate elephant seals that had infiltrated the living quarters that were reluctant to leave.

Armed with powerful laser beams the armed group climbed back over the fence following the trail, which led them to back the seal wallow.

"'I thought as much,' Ivan said to Tim who had also joined in the search. As they stood there in the misty swirling rain, their powerful beams of light raking back and forth across the muddy surface of the wallow, a lot of unusual movement beneath the surface caused the entire area to heave and swell before subsiding into a field of muddy bubbles. As they watched, one of those bubbles seemed to blink and stare into the light as though trying to make out what was beyond it.

"'My God, did you see that,' Dean whispered, 'something in there is watching us, let's get to hell out of here.'

"'Okay,' Ivan whispered, 'everyone back away from here, put the gear back in the field store and meet me in my quarters and not a word about this to anyone, from now on, this area is out of bounds to everyone.'

"Back in his office, the committee were briefed about what little they knew and it was decided to fence off the seal wallow and to erect an electric fence around the top of their security wall to stop any intruder from gaining access to the living quarters. Also, Wayne and Peter were dispatched to the radio room right now to set up the surveillance system. Adrian Moody a hobby farmer since his retirement and having been bitten once or twice, was known to have had first-hand experience with electric fences and he, along with a few willing helpers were given the task of erecting one. To keep whatever was in the wallow, in there… it was decided to fence it off with a strong wire mess security fence, which may or may not keep whatever it is, in there."

Chapter 16
A Meeting with The Unknown

By mid-morning the following day, an electric fence mounted on sturdy insulators, coupled to a large 1-mil Ω (Ohm's) capacitor completely surrounded the living quarters and an uneasy feeling settled over the station. Only those people required to leave the area for scientific studies were allowed out of the compound and although everyone tried to keep busy and not worry about it, each time someone went outside, they instinctively looked towards the seal wallow.

"Evening fell and the rain swirling across the well-lit area creating strange moving, dancing images, images that they normally would not have taken any notice of, but tonight it seemed that they had taken on a more sinister role.

"As Ivan stood at the rec-room door looking out into the swirling rain, from behind him someone called, 'You're wanted on the phone, Ivan,' and wiping the images from his mind walked to the bar and took up the receiver.

"'Hi there,' Ivan speaking he said.

"'Wayne here, Ivan,' a softly spoken voice said as though it did not want to be overheard. 'Something or some creature just left the seal wallow and is heading up your way. Did you get a good look at it mate?'

"'What does it look like?' Ivan asked.

"'You would not believe me Ivan, have a look for yourself, it is making for the side door of the powerhouse,' Wayne replied.

As he put the hand piece down the phone rang once more... picking it up enquired, 'What now Wayne?'

"'It's not Wayne, it's me Adrian, I am in the power house doing the 9 pm readings and we have a visitor, get yourself over here pronto, Oh and come alone.'

Grabbing an electric prod, Ivan ran to the powerhouse, letting himself in through the main entrance, made his way cautiously to the main office where Adrian was waving and pointing towards the console.

"Once in the office, he stared in the direction Adrian was pointing and there against the console was what Adrian described as a visitor. The best description would be that of a large oval silver coloured garden Slater or a multi legged parasite sometimes found on the tongue of a fish. It stood about 5 feet high with two round bulbous eyes mounted on long flexible stalks similar to that of a domestic snail. Its body was some sort of shiny metallic structure supported by several rows legs, which now hung loosely by its side. To complete the description, it had to large primary feelers with small pincers or scaly fingers on it, which waved menacingly back and forth.

"As they watched, the creature seemed quite un-perturbed by their presence as it busily scanned the electrical distribution console. They watched dumb founded, for as if it happy with what it saw, it started too rolled up in a ball and when it was bent over like a capitol A, it proceeded to stand on its hind quarters, straightened out and stood up straight.

"Turning to face them, its underside glowed crystal clear like a mirror and incredible as it seemed, Ivan was looking at a reflection of himself. As he looked, he began thinking, also seeing strange pictures and instruments as though he was seeing what the creature was thinking.

"'I think it is trying to convey something to us telepathically or by ESP,' Ivan whispered, 'Do you read it as well Adrian?'

"'Yes I do,' Adrian replied, 'but how the hell did it get a picture of me on its stomach?'

"'I have no idea,' Ivan replied, 'I can only see myself.'

"Concentrating on the strange apparition it seemed that they became part of it as images of galaxies, and planets, began to form with distant constellation sweeping past. They saw the interior of a highly sophisticated engine room, of ruptured bursting pipes, of exploding gaseous fireballs and heard weird cries and screams, and saw fleeting, disembodied apparitions floating in a liquid or vapour filled compartments. Figures that could only have been the crew of an alien space craft.

"Scenes of a strange saucer shaped craft racing headlong towards earth, then finally sitting on a column of fire thrusting out and down from the central-base of the vehicle arresting its headlong decent to destruction, it approached their island. Apparently having enough power to maintain control of the vehicle, it had hovered over the seal wallow, where standing on the column of fire, lights or laser beams blasted the edge of the wallow away, enlarging the hole big enough to allow the craft to settle down in to the depths of the Isthmus. As it sank into the sodden, muddy surface of the island, it continued to blow rocks and mud high into the air, until like an Echidna, it had disappeared from view. Finally, the water and mud seeped back into the wallow refilling it, effectively protecting it from the elements and hiding the vehicle from view.

"Five decades had passed since the vehicle malfunctioned and during that time, the crew after constructed a sliding roof to close over the wallow had successfully repaired their vehicle. Each spring during the breeding season, the roof would be opened and once it was full of seals happily wallowing and moulting in the mud the roof would slide silently closed trapping the seals beneath it.

"The fluid from these seals then became food for the crew who appeared to be of a cellular-particle form requiring only moisture and the gaseous CH^4 within a liquid shield, which apparently formed part of their support structure. They had no body as earth people knew and appeared to be part of the vehicle. With no protection against the earth's high atmospherical pressure of 14.7 psi, the aliens allocated to work outside the craft had the ability to mutate to another form. This enabled them to leave the craft in search of food and to stock the wallow with seal carcasses which once sealed under the sliding roof broke down to generate the essential supply of Methane gas which was then piped down into the craft's fuel cells.

"This Methane; used as part of the propellant in the power plant, guidance and stabiliser engines was also used to saturate the sealed crew compartment to create a living environment. However, the time taken to repair the craft and generating enough fuel to return home had created a catch 22 situations for the crew. Now after half century of rebuilding, while the craft was ready to fly, they had drained the electrical system and had no way of starting the main rotor system of their atomic Ion powered engine spinning. Secondly, the rich mixture of oxygen and methane now concentrated in the area immediately above the craft could destabilise the main engine once it was fired. Once ignited this flammable gaseous field could certainly hamper any lift off attempted. Therefore, the columns of fire in their thoughts reflected the suggestion that they wanted the gas immediately above the wallow burnt off before the craft could lift off safely through it.

"As Tim stared at the mutated creature, he wondered what it actually looked like before a scene at the wallow again over rode his thoughts. The area around it was opening up like a giant missile silo, the false top covered with mud, tussock grass, sleeping Gentoo penguins was moving up, and outwards to reveal a vast watery reservoir almost twice the original size of the wallow, beneath the surface the silvery sheen of the hull of their space vehicle could now be seen.

"As they watched the scene unfolding, at the edge of the wallow a pair of feelers reached up out of the mud to place what looked like a control panel out onto the dry ground and alongside it what appeared to be a spare coupling. This control panel housed a switch and a female electrical input socket, which apparently would accommodate the spare male plug lying alongside of it, all the while a vision of 400 Volts AC at 210 cycles load rating of 3000 Amperes kept coming and going in their vision and finally the vision of three suns sitting side by side.

"It was evident that to energise their craft, they would require a power supply for three days, and as we had nothing like their fittings it was also obvious that they were providing their own to re-wire our three-phase four-wire system to it. Normally we would not use a voltage or cycle setting of these high values, but if we isolated the station, shut everything down and brought the third engine on line, knowing that the engines could adequately carry such amperage (load), we could then recalibrate the consoles to that output.

"Looking towards the door the Alien looked back one last time and Ivan saw the planets in our solar system coming into line. Far out in deep space near the very edge of our own galaxy is the planet Uranus. The seventh in order from the sun and as though it was showing us where it came from, one of the small icy moons circling the planet lit up and glowed several times before receding to be lost once more in a galaxy of a billion stars. With the figure three foremost in our minds, the creature then turned and dropping down onto its legs scuttled out the side door.

"Phew", trying to come to terms with what they had just experienced, Ivan and Adrian looked at one another in disbelief. It was evident that the craft had experienced a fire or explosion inside the engine room or power plant, had subsequently lost both fuel and power, and had put down for repairs. Now that they had affected those repairs, generated enough methane fuel for food and fuel for the return voyage, they needed help by supplying electrical energy to start their machine. Finally, the figure three seemed to indicate that in three days their planet would be in line and that would be the last time for almost two centuries that the planet would be at the lowest point of its orbit around the earth again. Therefore, as they would never survive on earth, to miss this launch schedule could possibly signal their doomed so we had to start work tonight.

"This experience was too big; they could not keep it to themselves so after closing up the powerhouse they returned to the mess hall and summoned everyone to a special meeting. Looks of utter disbelief on the faces of the group were quite apparent…the fear of the unknown and even open scepticism was apparent within the group, but what could they do. To help them get off the island was as simply as supplying what they required, which was power and the vote was in favour of doing just that. We could not live with them and they who ever or whatever they were, could not exist here. Finally, for safety sake, except for those directly involved in the departure of the space vehicle, the rest of the group would stay within the safety of the compound.

"As nothing here on the station would work on the power factor they required, the first thing to do was to shut down every electrical appliance on the station. Wayne and Dean walked to the edge of the wallow and sure enough there sitting some distance back from the edge was a strange looking control board and a spare male four-pin plug. Returning the plug to the powerhouse, they examined it at great length, but none of them had ever seen anything like it in their life. They had no idea what sort of metal it was made from or whether we could attach our wiring to it, but as four variable clamps were attached to the short-staggered lengths of loom protruding from the back of the plug, it would seem that their thoughts had been pre-empted. Wayne attached a drum of three phase-four-wire cable to these and insulated each joint.

"The spare drum of cable was then rolled down the Isthmus trailing the power lead out behind it and the cable was connected to the control board at the edge of the wallow. Back up in the powerhouse the second and third engines were started and when normalised they were brought on line. As the powerhouse was now in darkness, using the beams of our torches, the manual over ride to the voltage output was readjusted to 400V and the cycles metre raised to 210 cycles. Once the space vehicle started to draw current, the three engines should be more than capable of carrying the anticipated 3000-Ampere load, which would drop off rapidly once the initial power surge passed and the craft started to generate its own power.

"At the powerhouse, in case of any voltage surge or feedback whether deliberate or not Wayne terminated the cable via a heavy card type, heavy capacity positive directional type diode heat sink complete with a fusible link before attaching the cable to the main circuit breaker. If we did experience any feedback whether deliberate or otherwise which could put us of the air forever within milliseconds this circuit would blow instantly like a domestic circuit breaker thereby protecting our own system. The other side of the anti-feedback circuit was then connected to the main circuit breaker in the power console.

"Once everything was in readiness, down by the seal wallow the extension lead was coupled to the control box and after a few moments a small red LED (Light Emitting Diode) blinked on and off several times indicating that they were ready to receive power. Tim pressed the contact button and by the sound of the three engines, labouring away up at the powerhouse, the craft had commenced drawing power. Stepping back behind the security fence the small group watched quietly as down in the depths of the wallow lights began to glow one after another. A high pitch whining followed the lights coming on and several whips like communication antennas speared up through the mud to wave back and forth in the swirling wind and rain.

"From the depths of the wallow, as the great cellular ion engine deep within the bowels of the craft began to spin, a high-pitched whining sound could be heard as the blowers or main rotor started to turn. As it spun faster and faster the louder and louder the whine became, until finally they were forced to put their hands over their ears to block out the noise. Once the noise level peaked, it settled back down to a deep throated, humming sound.

"From where the group stood near the seal barrier, it was obvious by the light pulsing on and off around the aerials or radio antennas that their radio communication system was on air, possibly trying to make contact with any other craft out there in deep space.

"As the engine of the vehicle run up to speed normalised and pre-flight checks were apparently being conducted, judging by the sound of our engines working hard to maintain the load, it was going to be a noisy old three days. However, after twenty-four hours, the load on the powerhouse dropped off to almost nil; they had stopped taking current. That same night, the sky above the station was lit by a series of brilliant lights shining down from a second space craft…lights, which illuminated all of north head and the entire isthmus as bright as daylight.

"As it hovered above North Head, the group responsible for the power ran down to the seal wallow only to find that the control panel was missing and their lead had been disconnected and thrown back away from the edge of the wallow. Rewinding the drum of cable the two standby engines were taken off line, allowed to normalise and the duty engine was re-calibrate to 240 Volts, 50 cycles and placed back on line. The circuit breaker was closed and once more, the station lit up like Lunar Lark.

"Then strangely, just after midnight on the third day after the electric fence had been erected, there was a brilliant flash and an un-earthly ear-piercing scream as something breached it. The lights around the station dimmed suddenly then glowed brightly once more as the engine on line lent over on its side taking the sudden load. Then, with the exception of the spacecraft hovering silently above North Head, all was quiet again…the engine on line recovered and settled down to a steady beat once more. A quick investigation by the group involved with the space craft evacuation found the electric fence around the station had not been breached, however inside the compound just beyond the rock wall a long crustacean like feeler with a bulbous eye on it, now lay on the damp sandy soil.

"Leaving it where it lay, the men armed with various weapons climbed over the fence and followed the tracks of the creature back to the wallow, here they found the strong wire mesh security fence pushed over and flattened like mosquito netting. Now that the craft was up to power, what was that creature doing coming up to the living quarters, was it going to deliver a message of thanks for their help… who knows? Yet it seemed strange and somehow hard to comprehend why a creature so technologically advanced would fall for something as simple as an old fashion electric fence? Now we would never know.

"Tonight, the mud within the wallow swirled and boiled like a witch's cauldron and in the total darkness of the Sub-Antarctic night, row upon row of lights could be seen shimmering away beneath the surface. Then as they watched in total disbelief, the scaly feeler, which had been left up in the compound had apparently developed rows of tiny legs and went scurrying past, slid down the wall of the wallow to disappear beneath the mud.

"Down below in the depths of the wallow, a light glowed brightly and went out again as though a hatch had been opened to admit the body part, a part which had made its own way home. Then the muddy surface began to brighten and dim, brighten and dim just like the little moon we had seen in our telepathic messages some days before. 'I think they are getting ready to leave,' Adrian suggested.

"'So do I,' Tim agreed.

"'Peter,' Ivan called, run back to the recreation-room and get that big hunting Bow from the display case and one arrow, 'Oh' and bind a sock or some rag to it; hurry.'

"'Alan,' he called again, 'get a can of petrol from the garage and an armful of cotton waste and bring it back here quickly…go, go, go.'

"Beneath their feet the giant volcanic conglomerate that was Macquarie Island, began to shimmy and vibrate as once more the outside edges of the seal wallow started to open outwards further away from the wallow, taking with it the remains of the fence. While far below the surface of the mud and water, a powerful force was being unleashed.

"'I think I know what it is,' someone called out aloud; 'it's a space vehicle alright.'

Trying not to sound too exasperated, Adrian replied, 'We know, we bloody know, we have been communicating with them remember, I hope you didn't think we have been talking to a large Elephant seal with a bad case of indigestion.'

"As the noise of the engine continued to increase, Alan and Peter arrived back at the wallow at the same time, Alan with an arm full of petrol-soaked rags and Peter with the bow.

"'Wet them with petrol and go around to the other side and throw the rags over the edge onto the surface of the wallow and get to hell out of there, if they are going to lift off now we have to burn off that methane,' Ivan called.

Then handing Dean the martial arts expert the bow, and as someone lit the petrol-soaked bundle of cloth on it he said, 'Aim for the rags on the far side of the wallow then drop flat on the grass, okay… Shoot.'

"Silhouetted against the pitch black of the Sub-Antarctic night, like a shooting star the flaming arrow raced across the seal wallow imbedding itself in the rags on the far side and as they dropped flat on the wet grass, the rags ignited and the accumulated methane gas above the wallow exploded skyward in a fiery ball. As the column of fire rolling inwards and upwards, extended high over the Isthmus to dissipate into the night sky, the roar and rumbling from deep within the wallow increased to an ear shattering, pulsing roar.

"As the top of the craft appeared above the mud, the communication antennas withdrew and the second spacecraft, which had been hovering above North Head, appeared directly above it. A brilliant beam of light descending through the dissipating smoke and flames to magnetically attach itself to the second craft as though it was going to help it overcome the suction created by the mud and assist it clear of its watery tomb.

"Spinning furiously a great disc shaped craft slowly appeared above the mud where assisted by its companion and standing on a column of fire or intense light, it lifted clear of the wallow into the night sky. Once free and apparently stable the intensity of the light from the second craft dimmed slightly but stayed attached as though still on standby. Then after a few moments of swinging from side to side like a spider on a web, the crew of the rescued craft apparently happy with its control over the vehicle took over complete control. The supporting light from the second vehicle faded altogether and in the blink of an eye, it disappeared to re-appear stationary over North Head once more. Left to its own devices the salvaged craft titled slightly and commenced rocking back and forth apparently still testing the controls. The lift off thrust jets had been switched off and now spinning silently like a child's top, it appeared to have nothing supporting it. Then without warning, it raced off to disappear into the Western Hemisphere, only to re-appear in a matter of seconds to hover over the mud-splattered group still lying on the centre of the isthmus. Once more sitting stationary on a beam of light, as it hovered motionlessly a small hatch on the underside-outside edge of the craft opened and a beam of light carried a small shimmering object down to the surface of the sandy isthmus.

"Once more, the humming noise of the engine grew louder and louder, the light went out and a large diaphragm similar to the shutter in a SLR camera opened in the base of the craft and a column of fire blasted down through it onto the earth, covering the prone onlookers in sand and debris. Then spinning furiously, it rose vertically up into the night sky, the column of fire roaring down from the base of it ceased, the hatch folded closed then titling slightly and closely followed by the second craft it raced upwards and away into the south west sector at an incredible rate to disappear in seconds."

Chapter 17
A Planet Beyond Our Time

Stunned by the experience, the Macquarie Island party lying partially buried beneath a thick layer of foul-smelling stinking mud and debris thrown off by the spinning craft as it had lifted clear of the wallow, stayed where they were for some time as they tried to come to terms with what they had just experienced. However, it was really beyond their comprehension. If that was a sample of visitors from outer space, then let them stay there where they belonged,

"'Any one for a shower?' A voice called.

"Getting to their feet, they trudged towards the living quarters, on the way they stopped and stared down at the strange crystal-like object that had been lowered from the rescued spacecraft, which now lay on the wet sand glowing on and off. The object was about the size of a large watermelon and powered by some unknown force it was aglow, brightening and dimming at a constant rate.

"'Do you think we ought to pick it up,' Ivan asked the group now gathered around it.

"'What the hell are you supposed to be,' someone enquired addressing the mysterious object, at which point the object brightened and a picture formed within it. It was a scene of the two space vehicles hurtling rapidly away from earth towards the distant edge of our known universe. As they travelled, fiery comets passed in and out of view, while like sparkling diamonds, meteorite showers hurtled past at an incredible pace and in the background, the earth became smaller and smaller. The object was in fact a though transference unit where you only had to think of something in the past or the future and it would preview the scene for you.

"In amazement, they stared at this incredible gift as it recounted their epic voyage from Australia and saw the 'Polly Woodside' on the high seas, the fishing and the loss of two of their colleagues, now very vividly shown being taken by sharks. As they watched, they witnessed the craft passage past Mars, Venus, Jupiter and the fiery rings around Saturn. Approaching Uranus, it veered towards the outer edge of our galaxy and approached a smaller constellation of several smaller planets all linked by a common circular ring of gaseous substances, probably nitrogen or methane. Approaching one of the planets within the group, both craft commenced a controlled descend down through cloudless atmosphere towards the surface.

"They watched in disbelief, as the vehicles entered the lower atmosphere towards the barren ice covered-featureless surface of this unknown planet. There were no seas, land mass's or mountain ranges, just an ice-covered surface surrounded by a swirling gaseous field of some kind. The closer the craft came to the surface the more apparent was it that it was now homing on an IRS location signal emitted from below the vapour level.

"Entering and passing through the vapour shield, the craft re-appeared beneath it above a field of pulsing lights surrounding a deep chute or silos. Centring the craft over the chute and beaming out several guidance beams from the periphery or rim of the craft, it fixed itself in the centre of the chute and once stabilised, dropped quickly beneath the surface of the planet to hurtle downwards towards home.

"Within the core of the planet at a predetermined time the retro system fired arresting the downward plunge of the craft, it slowed and coming to a halt, came to rest on a platform located immediately beneath the chute. After shutting down the main motive system it was whisked away to be replaced by another receiver and finally deported at what appeared to be a service control centre. There it passed through a decontamination centre which scoured the outside of the craft of any bacterial spores which may have contaminated it during the long years submerged beneath earth's crust or indeed picked up in the solar system.

"Before moving it on to a reception area, the fuel system was pumped out and discharged out into space into the gaseous shield surrounding the planet. It is quite possible that this same fuel was recovered when re-fuelling an expedition vehicle. It was strange, that although many other craft were quite obvious in this area, there were no apparent ground staff or crews. Every action was mechanical. At reception, a metal tube appeared out of a stark white wall and attached itself to a small fitting in an open hatch in the crew quarters. Lights flashed and a high-pitched noise similar to that of a domestic vacuum cleaner was quite evident as the vapour and cellular forms of the crew within the control compartment were purged from the craft.

On the other side of the wall, the vapour from the crew compartment went through a de-fragmentation system and the fragmented cellular bodies of the crew were separated from their life support vapour. The crew now reformed and under their own power moved through decontamination centre before finally entering the de-briefing centre where thought projection automatically received and stored the data from their epic voyage. It also instigated remedial action to counter any similar systems failure, which had caused their craft to malfunction. Then finally, the crew moved out onto a parapet that over looked their home, a home situated within the very core of the planet.

"As the inhabitants of Macquarie Island watched in amazement, through the eyes of one of the crew they received a panoramic view of life within the core of the planet. There were no great cities, inspiring buildings or monuments. There were no rivers or parks, no seas or mountains, simply a sterile white honeycomb lining, which covered the entire inside of the core. This lining had millions of tiny openings in it like honey comb, which apparently housed the inhabitant, factories and food/vapour generation systems.

There were no marvellous space vehicle concepts or cargo carrying Anti-Gravitational Vehicles moving silently past. As each of the inhabitants possessed the ability to project themselves to any destination by thought transference and as they lived on the moisture/nutrient enriched vapour generated here within the core, which they absorbed through a gill like membrane, there was no need of farms, bovine or other products that required heavy craft for transportation. The scene was one of total sterility, nothing that the human mind could come to terms with and whether or not it was deliberate, none of the crew looked at the other so those viewing the scene, had no idea of what the inhabitants of this strange planet looked like.

Was it important that we see what they looked like?

Alternatively, were we ready to see so far into the future?

"'A thousand years from now this little gadget will be a great house hold item,' Tim said looking at his father, 'but for now I don't think we really need it, do you?'

"'No,' Ivan replied, 'let's commit it to the seal wallow where this all started, who knows one day when there is a drought down here some future explorer or archaeologist may stumble across it and a future world will know us as we were today.'

"Thrown out into the middle of the wallow, the shimmering crystal lay on the thick muddy surface for some time before slowly sinking. As it slowly sank out of sight the top of the wallow lit up brightly, the misty rain creating a hologram or screen that showed several small cosmonauts dressed in strange pressurised garb with one of their many arms raised in a farewell salute, only to fade quickly as the crystal sank. The eerie glow dimmed and went out forever."

Chapter 18
Getting on With Life

"The months following the space craft incident past quickly and it was soon put behind them. While with the impending spring, the indigenous fauna would once more return to the isthmus, the gentoo penguins waddling happily about with a beak full of tussock grass began to make a new nest, also the elephant seals who would finally return not only to the isthmus, but also the great wallows to moult.

"Once the future inhabitants of the outlying station were agreed upon, the bulk of the up grading completed and the various stores, foodstuffs and clothing had been allocated, as weather permitted, the distribution of these stores would start.

"As the last few weeks of winter set in all its fury, the endemic inhabitants of the island had long since left on their annual migration to warmer northern regions or out onto the great Antarctic convergence at latitude 64 to feed on the abundance of food along the great convergence.

"During this time, the main living area under North Head outwardly appeared closed up. However, while it may have looked like that on the outside; inside nothing could have been further from the truth. In fact, it was quite the opposite, in many ways. It was as industrious as an ant's nest with the member of the various groups allocated to the many outstations around the island, feverishly learning new skills. They divided and commenced to grow new yeast plants for bread and beer making. Learnt first aid and Midwifery skills. Finally packing what personal items they had, for with the coming spring a new and exciting episode in the lives of the inhabitants was to unfold.

"In readiness for what was to be a very busy schedule, the little sealer chapel, which had with stood the elements for over 2·5 centuries, was cleaned and repainted. Inside, the Padre hung Holy pictures and religious trappings adorned the altar and the walls. For apart from normal church services and Sunday school, the first recorded marriage on the island, would soon be conducted there.

"As the world and everything they once knew had been taken from them, each of these forthcoming weddings would be an individual affair, complete with all the 'Old World' trimmings. Each bride and groom would have their own special day with all the cherished memories that would be theirs alone to share for all time with each of these weddings followed by a week's honeymoon at Bauer Bay R-R resort.

"As the sun had long since set on that first long winter's night, like scenes from a picture postcard series, snow filled gales now swept continuously across the island covering the mountaintops and the high plateau region with snow. On the Isthmus, snow devils raced joyfully in and around the living quarters covering everything in a soft mantle of cold white snow. Surrounding the communal square, strings of multicolourful lights were run around the outside all the buildings. Not as though the darkness or the swirling snow storms worried them, but the fact that they had so much to do before the sun came up again, that the outside lights simply added a festival atmosphere, making each day during the long months of darkness, just that little more enjoyable.

"The livestock, had been brought down from the high country to the lower levels along the protected eastern foreshore and housed in specially constructed stone corrals sealed with mud complete with a thatched tussock grass and mud roof to keep out the cold blustery drafts. Here they were confined during bad weather and let out to eat and drink whenever there was a break in the weather. Once let out to feed, the herds were grazed up along the protected lower eastern slopes of the island between the station and Gadgets Gully.

"Now that winter had almost run its course another very important task to make sure that it did not ice over, was to check the new fresh water catchment area up on the plateau at the head of Gadgets gully. Also, that the temperature in the main water storage tanks was constantly monitored, for it would be disastrous if the water were to freeze and the expanding ice cracked the Ferro concrete tanks, not to mention wrecking the pumps and fittings.

"As previously mentioned, the main community hall comprised two rooms, a generous kitchen, and the large dining room-come recreation room complete with bar area, cinema, pool tables and lounge chairs. The kitchen had a long workbench and sink on the northern wall, a very large oil fired stove with four ovens. A walk-in pantry and two more workbenches on the eastern and western walls. It was well fitted out with a large dough-mixing machine for making bread, an industrial bread slicer and a domestic refrigerator, along with all the various types of useful cooking appliances.

"It was here within the warm friendly atmosphere of the kitchen away from the howling shrieking wind, the drifting snow and darkness, that cooking classes were conducted. Also, cakes and sweets for the forth-coming wedding would be prepared, and not forgetting the preparation of the homemade beer before it was removed to the brewery to ferment.

"Life within the main station had settled down to an orderly well-oiled routine, even if it was not your every day run of the mill type suburban routine. Working in rotating shifts the older women controlled the kitchen and ran the mess or dining room; they prepared the meals and conducted cooking classes. Rostered shifts of older girls and boys, assisted by setting up and clearing away the tables in the mess before and after meals, finally washing and polishing the mess area, this took a lot of pressure off those preparing so many meals.

"After breakfast each day, those not employed in the mess, would disappear to his or her appointed place of work or study, for every inhabitant of this remote society, each new day brought a whole new way of life. Wayne taught radio communications and maintenance down in the radio shack: Peter and Matthew, as well as one of the teachers from the MacFarlane clan taught primary and secondary school levels as well as technical studies and Engineering in one of the large scientific rooms in the former Science block.

"Ivan and Mitta Moody instructed the newly inducted mechanical apprentices, both boys and girls, as diesel mechanics, the operation of the powerhouse, covering power generation, distribution and repairs. In the main workshop, which is situated down on the Isthmus, this same mechanical group had commenced production of the first, high capacity 240-volt wind generator.

"Robbin the doctor had taken several medical trainees under his wing, and set about the meticulous task of educating them in all aspects of Medical Science, these trainees would be our future doctors, medical staff and SAR, and in time would assist in running the hospital and medical clinics situated in the various smaller settlements around the island.

"Future brides who were not on duty or at training schools, cluttered around the most popular lady on the island, Alan's wife 'Dorthe' who was a seamstress-come dressmaker. Was designing and manufacturing clothing not only for themselves but also for the future generation they would bring into the world. Curtains and bedding, tablecloths and personal items, which they would soon need to set up their own home when they settled in of the outlying stations during the coming spring, clothing and haberdashery that buzzed out from below the rapidly moving sowing machine needle.

"As material for patterns were at a premium, most of the designing and pattern work were completed on assorted mediums such as old pieces of canvas, cardboard taken from food and packing cases, or stiff brown paper and thin plastic sheeting when it was available. Once a design was settled on, the pattern was stored on computer hard drive and a copy on 30 Gb memory sticks for future use. Life was at last full and exciting for the young ones, with each day bringing a new challenge and a new experience. Exciting – yes, but in some cases also very dangerous for this majestic island so silent and aloof, so green and spectacular; was also like a funnel web spider; lying quietly, unseen, patiently waiting for its victim.

"One morning, after letting the stock out to graze along the steep eastern wall of the Island between the razorbacks opposite Buckles Bay and Gadgets Gully where the grass was abundant. Teelah and Angie, the two adopted feral girls along with Dominic and Aubrey herded them high up along the eastern wall. When without warning, some of the deer decided to make a dash for the high plateau country and freedom.

"Unfortunately, for them, the broad cabbage weed and tall almost impenetrable Tussock grass, which grew in abundance as high as a man's shoulder along the steep mountainside impeded their progress. To cut off their line of escape, Teelah raced up ahead of them and turned them back down towards the shoreline. Standing alone on the high slope she watched their antics with delighted, as they leapt, hopped, jumped and fell on their nose's in the tall grass in their mad headlong dash back down the steep slope.

"In case they decided to head south along the rocky foreshore, Teelah decided to descend via a nearby steep scree slope to cut them off. A scree slope is simply a narrow chute made up of millions of tiny pebbles about the size of a marble and as you descend in it, it all starts to run with you, until finally you are knee deep in it and running like mad to keep your balance. In this manner, it takes only a few seconds to descend one or two hundred feet.

"Half way down the slope, Teelah picked up her right foot and as she took the next rapid step, she put her foot down on a sheet of black ice. Slipping in the running pebbles, she fell backwards flat of her back with her left leg trapped beneath her body. Carried now by the moving, running scree slope, she slid rapidly down to the base the slope where her outstretched right leg struck the rocks bordering the beach.

The force of the impact bucketing the cartilage out of and around the knee joint. A brilliant flash of pain, and comforting darkness settled over her as she fell unconscious.

"Protected from the pounding sea behind the line of rocks, Teelah was also hidden from those searching along the narrow foreshore. Dominic, Teelah's fiancé and co-worker was back towards the station on the northern side of the slope that she had come down, so he had no idea where she was, nor in fact that she was seriously hurt. However, as he knew that she was more than capable of looking after herself, it did not really worry him when he could not see her.

"As the visibility became worse, the mob became increasingly restless; Dominic and the other pair of helpers decided to herd the flock back into their corral for the time being and after rounding them up, moved north along the foreshore towards the station. Looking back now and then Dominic half-expecting Teelah to appear out of the fog and after jumping playfully on his back would ride him into the sand for a quick wrestle and a hug. However, by the time they had reached the corral and herded the animals safely inside, Dominic was now really worried; Teelah had not returned.

"Closing the gate on the stock, they ran to the radio shack and after raising the alarm, the S.A.R team quickly appeared on the scene. Following Dominic, Robbin the Doctor with a stretcher and the medical team, hurried south towards the distant grazing area. Mother Nature; as though protecting one of her own had created the thick blanket of fog, which drifting quickly in off the ocean, blanketing the island and the mountain sides alike, at the same time it also covered the unconscious form of Teelah, now lying helpless against the rocks.

"Knowing that the vast majority of the large birds on the island were carnivorous scavengers, Ivan was thankful for the fog. He knew that it would hide her from the birds on their never-ending beach patrol, for unable to protect herself from the razor-sharp beaks of the large northern and southern giant retrels (Macronettes Halli), the Dominican gulls or skuas, Teelah could be maimed or blinded in a very short period.

"He also felt that if she had fallen, she would most probably be found somewhere down by the edge of the foreshore. However, a search of the area between the Razor back ridge and Gadgets Gully prove futile, she was simply not there. Scouring the mountain side up to and over the edge and onto the plateau, the party also searched beneath the massive clumps of tussock grass and under the broad leaves of the cabbage weed, but to no avail, it seemed as though Teelah had simply vanished.

"Moving further south Tim eventually came to the foot of the scree slope and noticed that ice still bordered both edges yet loose dry stones were quite evident down the centre and knowing the stock would not cross it, something else must have disturbed it; could it have been Teelah?

"Making his way down the edge of it searching under the undergrowth as he went, then as though some one was watching over her, the sea fog lifted abruptly and now visible there, laying against the rocks, was Teelah's crumpled body.

"'I've found her,' Tim shouted at the top of his voice, 'over here at the foot of the scree slope, hurry…bring the Doc.'

From person to person the called echoed along the mountainside.

"'They have found her; she is down at the foot of the screen slope.'

Once on the scene, Robbin covered her inert form with a space blanket to generate some warmth and to keep her warm, then slowly yet methodically he checked her out.

"'She appears okay, just unconscious for the time being,' he said. 'I can't see or feel any obvious injury, let's get her onto the stretcher and back to hospital where I can carry out a more detailed examination.'

"'Careful with her, it looks like her legs could be hurt,' Doc said as he slowly straightening out her left leg, which until now had been trapped beneath her body. 'Okay let's get her onto the stretcher and make her as comfortable as possible," and with four people each side, Teelah was gently lifted and place on the stretcher. The cover was replaced and once secured to the stretcher by broad safety straps to stop her falling off, she was lifted clear of the slope, out over the rocks and carried down onto the beach.

"As though she knew that Teelah, the child of the forest was now safe, Mother Nature in long trailing fingers carried the last traces of the thick fog far out to sea towards the distant horizon. Once more overhead, Southern Giant Petrels, the vultures of the sea were as they glided silently past on their eternal beach patrol, totally unaware that dinner was being carried far beyond their reach.

"Back at the hospital, Teelah's clothing was removed and she was covered with a medical gown, you know one of those short white glamour gowns, which always seem so very impersonal and never fit. They leave your bare bum sticking out the back and tries its level bloody best to strangle you and of course; and of course, rarely if ever fit. A full examination, body CT scan and X-ray's, showed only a damaged cartilage in her right knee. The diagnosis, it would have to come out otherwise she would be crippled.

"As the continual movement of her legs, the voices, the strange humming of the CT machine and systems scanners slowly penetrated her subconscious, Teelah opened her eyes to a strangely unfamiliar sterile-world of white. As though the feral instinct of yesterday had suddenly re-surfaced, her eyes narrowed to slits like a cornered dingo as she scanned the scene searching for an avenue of escape; it was the look of a hunted animal.

"Dominic, who was standing back out of the way, yet watching everything like a hawk, sensed the sudden fear and anxiety in his future bride, a bride that was now seemingly trapped in an unfamiliar, hostile world.

"'Wanna loan of me, Harley to get out of here?' he drawled casually approaching the operating table and squeezing her hand to gently re-assure her.

"'What's wrong with me?' she asked looking furtively from left to right.

"'Where am I? Why won't my legs work? Why?'

"'If you will just shut up for a bloody minute I will tell you,' Dominic said patiently, 'now first, did you come down the scree slope?'

"'Yes,' she replied, 'I did and I must have stepped on some black ice and slipped, the last thing I remember was sliding down the slope towards the Rocks.'

"'Well, I have some good news for you, you reached them all right, but the bad news is you have damaged one of your front forks, which shows you're a bloody idiot,' Dominic said as though he was taking about his beloved Harley Davidson motor bike.

Sounding somewhat exasperated Teelah shouted, 'I haven't got front forks you idiot, I've got bloody legs.'

"'Well, that makes it easier to explain then,' said Dominic patiently, 'one of them is busted and the Doc is going to fix it.'

"'Okay.'

"'Now, I will stay here and watch over you and you just do as the Doc say's, alright, we have to be able to walk out of here to our new home when the sun comes up, remember?'

"'Okay,' Teelah replied, 'but don't you go away, just give me a kiss ya big lug and wait for me to wake up, okay?'

"As though they had been doing it all their lives, the newly trained medical team professionally prepared her for the theatre and soon it was time to go under.

"'Now,' Robbin said in his most professional bedside manner, 'I'm going to put a little needle in the back of your hand, it might sting a bit but then you will feel nice and warm and will go off to sleep, when you wake up it will be all over.'

"'Okay.'

"'Right, oh, then here we go.'

"The small needle did prick and it certainly did sting slightly as it was inserted into the vein on the back of her hand and as she lay there listening to all the garbled talk, like can you count to ten for me. Of course she could count to ten, what did Robbin think she was, an idiot? The stinging sensation soon passed and not only did Teelah feel warm and comfortable, but also saw that some idiot had put her in the base of a tall glass tube and way up at the top of it the sun was looking down over the rim laughing down at her.

"*What a stupid looking sun*, she thought as she started to climb up the tube towards it, but just as she reached it and was about to grab it by the throat, it went *'pop'* and she woke up.

"From somewhere out in space, a familiar voice said, 'Stop shaking your bloody head and lay still.'

"'Water,' Teelah croaked, 'someone give me a drink of water.' Yet plead as she may, her cries fell on deaf ears.

"'Dominic,' Teelah called, 'please get me some water, I can't swallow.'

"'Leave her alone,' Doc said sternly as he moved towards the bedside, 'to give her anything now will do her more harm than good. I will moisten her lips and tongue with a sponge in a minute.'

"The relief of having her parched lips moistened with the damp sponge was enough for her to drift back into the comforting pain free arms of Morpheus the Goddess of Sleep.

"When Teelah finally awoke, the day had passed and the mournful sound of the night wind welcomed her back to the land of the living, she was safe and sound and all tucked up in bed in the patient's room. A glucose/saline drip had been inserted in the back of her left hand and a large cool, tantalising jug of fresh water stood looking smugly at her from the side locker.

"The auto-surgical suction unit had examined, operated on and successfully removed the ruptured cartilage. Once this was done, it was then replaced it with a synthetic cartilage to stop the bones rubbing together and to increase the healing process. Only a few strap marks where the machine had been attached, a small scar with four stitches on the inside of her right knee were the only indication that she had ever been operated on.

"Time moved relentlessly forward and only 12 hrs after the operation Teelah was fitted with a leg manipulator that slowly stretched and bent her leg in and out. Slowly at first then as each hour past it increased in speed until the knee and was bent and extended at a normal walking pace. After some hours the manipulator was removed, Robbin sat her up, swivelled her around and left her with both legs dangling over the side of the bed.

"'Oh Boy, the pain,' she muttered.

"'I know it is stiff and I know it is very sore,' Doc said in his best bed side manner; 'however I want you to try and swing your legs back and forth for me.'

"'It won't move,' Teelah pleaded.

"'What do you mean, it won't move?' Dominic mimicked, dismissing her protests. Yet, try as she may, she just could not move that leg, the right one was fine but the left one just hung down like the limb of a dead tree. Great big crocodile tears rolled down her cheek as she tried desperately to move it. But it did not move an inch.

"'Ya wanna get carried down the aisle?' a familiar voice enquired. Looking around Teelah spotted Dominic leaning nonchalantly against the wall.

"'No, I don't wanna get carried down the aisle as you so crudely put it,' she replied angrily between sobs.

"'Well,' Dominic said casually, as he walked up and stood in front of her, 'if you're not going to put it into gear and see if it will move, we have just wasted a lot of time giving it a major overhaul.'

"'I'm not a bloody motor bike, it isn't a front fork and I didn't have a new shocker fitted, I'm a girl and in case you haven't noticed it's a bloody leg,' Teelah said kicking out at him in sheer frustration.

"'Oh God, the pain,' she cried out as she unconsciously kicked out with the wrong leg.

"'There you are, I told you it would work,' Dominic said grinning from ear to ear. He was perfectly aware that it was a leg and a darn good looking one at that.

"'Just you wait, Dominic Hawthorn,' Teelah sobbed, 'Just you bloody wait.'

"*Boy*, Dominic thought, as he gave her a re-assuring hug, *that girl sure picked up the Australian lingo quickly*.

Like the Lord, on the third day Teelah rose again and with the aid of a walking frame, took the first few painful steps. As one day quickly followed another she graduated from the frame to half crutches, then to a walking stick and finally the arm of a loved one; Yep, she was away again in fact you would have thought she was Jana Pittman, marvellous what the thought of a forthcoming Olympic event or a wedding can do!

"During winter as snow now covered the island. The snowfalls had created a whole new dimension to the scene. 'Tobogganing', the younger set dragging their hastily constructed toboggans up razor back ridge, played and skied down the northern wall of the plateau into a secluded hidden valley above the ridge. Here in the relative safety of these protected gentle slopes, they let off a lot of steam, not to mention a lot of wrestling mixed with intimate bonding."

Chapter 19
The Great Day

"As Emma, the first bride of this unique community, dressed and readied for her wedding, Mother Nature had joined in the festivities lighting the night sky with a dazzling display of great southern lights. Brightly coloured auroras, raced back and forth across the island towards the Antarctic continent or hung momentarily over the island in great colourful waving hanging curtains of fire that lit the night sky like day. David the bridegroom was on powerhouse duties that day and once his shift finished headed for the shower; but try as he may, using soap, detergent, cologne and powder, he still smelt vaguely familiar, in fact just like an old empty 44-gallon fuel drum.

"Well, she is just going to like me as I am, he thought, desperately cleaning some stubborn grease from under his fingernails.

"Tonight, of all nights, snow fell freely and the large fluffy white flakes whipped up by the wind, swirled and danced around the living quarters as if they too wanted so badly to be part of this historical event. Here in a world totally devoid of personal transport, there were no stretched AVG for the bride, the bride's maids or the flower girls. Yet, far removed from civilisation, the old Aussie/ Italian initiative had come to the fore.

"Working tirelessly for many weeks out of sight in the main garage, Alvario had constructed a carriage, just like Cinderella's coach. This coach fitted neatly into the small trailer, which normally carried the small bulk fuel tank used to refill the oil heaters around the station as well as the kitchen stove. Tonight however, it had been transformed into a magical, romantic carriage, just as Cinderella had used on her way to the Prince's Ball.

"Inside the quaint little Sealers chapel, as canned music played selected hymns the entire community sat patiently awaiting the arrival of the bride. While up front to the right of the little altar, The Padre, David the bridegroom and Aub as the best man, waited patiently. *'Putt, putt, putt',* the unmistakable sound of the very ancient little Massey Ferguson tractor could be heard over the mournful howling, wailing of the night wind or… was it the night wind. Outside, as the living quarters were suddenly illuminated in a dazzling blaze of multi-coloured lights, it was obvious that it was not the wind, but a large spacecraft hovering high above the bridal party, creating a whole new dimension on the wedding. It seemed that since their departure, the space voyagers had been monitoring the lives of those that had rescued them and today had returned to share this historical human experience, an experience totally foreign to them.

Then as the canned music burst forth with "Here comes the bride", the door opened to reveal the bridal party. A flower girl minus the flowers but instead carrying a ring on a lace cushion. The bride's maid's and the glowing bride decked out in long trailing traditional bridal gowns of the 19th century looking as radiant as any bride could wish, entered on the arm of her father Alan. As the door was pushed closed against the wind, a small spinning orb entered and hovered up against the back wall, it was apparent that the visitors were going to preserve or transmit this moment.

As the spiritual wedding service conducted by the Padre drew to a close,

"'Would you all stand?' he asked while looking towards the strange coloured ball of light hovering silently on the rear wall of the chapel.

"We are gathered here in the sight of God and you here present, to join together in holy wedlock this man and this woman. Should there be any one present who knows any legal impediment why these two people should not be joined together in holy wedlock, let them now speak or forever hold his piece.'

"No reply.

"'Do you, James, smelling somewhat of stale fuel oil, take thee Emma Louise Hawthorn to be your lawful wedded wife, to have and to love and to hold from this day forth, for better or for worse; in sickness and in health until death do you part.'

"'I do.'

"'Do you, Emma, take thee, David as your lawful wedded husband, to have and to hold, from this day forth, for richer or poorer, in sickness and in health for better or for worse from this day forth.'

"'I do.'

"'David… Emma take this ring as a token of my love and affection I thee wed, and slid the ring on her finger, in the name of the Father, the Son and the Holy Spirit.'

"'Ivan... By the powers invested in my by the Shire of Esperance in the State of Tasmania, I now pronounce you man and wife and will leave it up to you to work out who is who! David... you may now kiss the bride.'

"'I knew it,' someone remarked, 'he just couldn't bloody resist it.'

"As the wedding breakfast swung into top gear, no amount of sleet or drift snow could have had the slightest effect on the festival atmosphere that permeated the great mess hall. Music played, toasts were made and finally every one sat down to the wedding breakfast. As in day's gone bye, traditional wedding photos were taken; toasts to the bride and parents were made. Telegrams especially written as though from distant relatives and friends were read out, and the wedding cake was cut. Music played the Bridal waltz, they dance until dawn, and all the while, the little spinning ball hovered un-obtrusively high up in the ceiling.

"As the first grey tinge of dawn lit the eastern horizon, the music slowed, the party ground to a halt and a new chapter in the life of the community was about to unfold. For the newlyweds, there was no bridal car, no tins tied on the back bumper, and no. 'Just married' written in red lipstick on the new duco.

Nope, the going away outfit was a sturdy set of waterproof quarpel combinations with waterproof Canadian hunting boots and a serviceable hat too shed the rain. Not forgetting of course, the his and hers matching 'Carrymore' Hi-packs loaded with their own personal gear as well as safety equipment for the trek to the honeymoon suite at Bauer Bay.

"The wedding breakfast over, David and Emma appeared in their his and hers travelling clothes and after walking the gauntlet of hugs and kisses hoisted their backpacks and securing the broad waistband then hand in hand struck out down the compound. As they walked, the spacecraft was still hovering silently above the isthmus and as it opened a small hatch to retrieve the spinning orb, Emma stop and looking up at it called.

"'If I spot you mob sticky beaking over at Bauer Bay, I will shoot you down, do you get the message?' And, as if the occupants understood the threat of bodily harm, the craft swung gently from side to side in acknowledgement, before lifting up and within seconds disappeared.

"As the spring sun had not yet risen, the cold biting morning wind quickly chilled their fingers, so they didn't walk hand in hand for very long, an impromptu stop and on with the mittens and gloves. Then it was up over the protective rock wall separating the station from the isthmus, around the odd torpid elephant seal that had forgotten to go to sea or had arrived back on the island early. Past the last few remaining wet, bedraggled looking gentoo penguins… on past the radio shack where they knocked on the window and waved to Wayne and the radio crew as they passed. On past the met section, the garage and scientific blocks and finally past an old weathered sign, which stood in the middle of the tussock covered isthmus and simply read, 'Please don't feed the Scientists.'

"At the southern end of the isthmus, they took the doctor's track up the razor back ridge, a ridge that rose a mile or more to the plateau region. This track, which runs along the very top of the ridge, which shaped like a capitol A takes its name from an original ANARE expedition, doctor who lost a few marbles during an expedition back in the 20th century. He supposedly carried a director's chair up here and would sit in a shallow depression hidden in the tall tussock grass and spy on the station below. To add spice to the situation, some say he also had a rifle with him and that made things quite interesting for people going about their daily tasks down on the isthmus far below.

"Buffeted by the gale force westerly winds, which were shrieking up over the unprotected ridge, the couple finally cleared the track and once up on the shoulder of the unprotected plateau, headed southwest towards the top of the island. Stopping every so often to admire the view, a look into the heavens for a spacecraft or any one that might be following, as well as to regain their breath. From up here they could see far to the east, as well as far out over the restless grey sea to the west, where the feeble rays of the winter sun tried desperately to shine through the fleeting rain and snow squalls. A quick hug and a kiss and then off again.

"After a long hard slog, they eventually reached the broad open expanse of the plateau region on the very top of the island. Up here although open to the ravages of the weather, there is no known cover, grass, shrubs or trees of any sort, the going was much easier as the made their way along a well-defined path that meandered in and around the many shallow lakes and tarns that dotted this section of the featureless plateau.

"Finally, high above the western side of the island they stopped to take in the view, a view that can only be seen through the eyes of young lovers. They watch in awe at the fury of the sea and the huge waves that crashed as far as the eye could see along the entire boulder strew western foreshore. Mist and spray from the tumultuous waves blowing inland towards the base of the steep mountains, which rose up out of the vast tundra or feather bed region between the rocky foreshore and the mountains. Normally it would have been a scene of utter desolation, but today in the eyes of the beholders the awesome might and power of Mother Nature, was a scene of raw savage beauty.

"Crossing the island to the west, they came to the edge of the plateau and looked down on Bauer bay, which was situated behind a broad open beachfront at the base of a descending valley. Bauer Bay lies nestled on the floor of a broad green valley and is bordered on three sides by the steep mountains to the north, east and south, and to the west is open to the only rock free beach on this side of the island. The buildings, which make up this resort, sit at the very front of the valley closest to the beach while behind and home to hundreds of rabbits, small rolling open grass covered verges and depressions, covered several acres.

"In front of them the well-worn path made its way down the base of a sheltered valley and came out onto the flat sandy beach a quarter of a mile or so from the building. Here a torrent of fresh water only a few inches deep and several hundred yards wide ran quickly toward to pounding surf. Oblivious to the wind, the swirling rain and the mist from the sea, the bubbling, running water dashing madly towards the sea and the crashing of the waves, which waited eagerly to devour it, the happy couple finally reached the resort and opening the door entered, and quickly closed the door on yesterday and the elements alike. For them, life was about to begin.

"With the closing of the door, as though insulated form the world outside, time suddenly stood still. The roar of the pounding surf and the hiss of the receding water became an orchestrated symphony of love. While the rain, which had now really settled in-in earnest created moving, swishing, ever-changing scenes and patterns on the large exposed windowpane.

"For many weeks prior to her wedding, Emma with Teelah for company had been coming over to the resort to decorate it and set the interior up to suit herself. Fresh clean sheets and covers adorned the bridal bed; frilly lace curtains on the once naked windows added that personal touch, which today belonged only to them. As they removed their wet garments and softly towelled one another dry, they were oblivious to the cold interior of the building and there was no mad rush to light the heaters.

"Searching and exploring one another before hopping in between the cool fresh sheets where they were totally oblivious to the cold bedding or the thundering surf, and there serenaded by Mother Nature they melted into one another. Setting the seal on their tomorrow and somewhere during the afternoon, the seed was sown and a fertile egg now snuggled tightly on the rich fertile wall of the virginal womb. Whatever the future had in store; on this day, the new generation of Macquarie Islanders had begun.

"As the late afternoon sun tried desperately to break through the fleeting storm clouds, the passing storm abated and the roar and hiss of the sea faded. Like a beacon, a light flickered off and on through the window of the resort to settled down to shine brightly, while above the building a thin column of smoke rose lazily from the chimney.

"The exciting days of exploring not only themselves but also their island home was theirs to cherish and remember.

Daily excursions took them far from Bauer Bar, playing along the rugged western coastline, picking up ancient artefact and old glass floats that were once used at sea by the Japanese on long line fishing before they were banned. The eerie feeling experienced when entering Mawson's or Auroral caves and looking with a heavy heart at the fossilised bones of hundreds of unfortunate Wandering Albatross Chicks which had been killed and eaten by the early sealers here in this cave.

"Here and there along the rocky promontories and outcrops, hundreds of Blue Eyed cormorants or king shags after a morning at sea fishing stood with their wings outstretched to dry. Indeed an exercise in futility in the steadily pouring rain. Now and then they stopped too cuddle into one another for warmth and watch the majestic waterfalls flooding off the lip of the plateau high above them, to tumble hundreds of feet down to the tundra below. Together, they sat on the high walls of Petrel Peak watching the angry sea break over the submarine reef that extended south to Judge and Clerk Islands. Alternatively, spent many memorable hours watching the majestic Grey Headed Albatross sitting sedately on the nests. Or the colourful array of sea birds wheeling in and out high above the turbulent sea practising ritual mating displays as a prelude to the coming mating season. While light Mantled Sooty Albatross performing incredible feats of ritual paired flights past along the face of the cliffs.

"Down by the sea on small rocky Islets in Windsor Bay, they stopped to admire the incredibly beautiful Black Browed Albatross chick sitting stiffly aloof on their silly looking truncated cone shaped nests of mud and grass. Alternatively, lay on the damp grassy slopes of the amphitheatre watching the antics of the large Wanderer chicks standing on the lip of their nest, flapping their great wings while strengthening their muscles in preparation for their imminent departure, or simply preening themselves while filling in time patiently waiting a parent to return with food.

"As they lay there quietly watching the Albatross chicks, dozens of cheeky little field mice having made their burrows in the walls of the nest, scampered quickly by in search of what precious little seed could be had. Totally oblivious of the young couple, they foraged under the broad leaves of the cabbage plants, collecting the dry wind-blown seed trapped there and after packing it in their cheek pouches would scurrying out of site to store it in their burrows. As each precious day faded the couple would make their way up onto the plateau where hand in hand, or snuggled up to one another out of the chilling wind, head for the warmth and comfort of Bauer Bay.

"Today however, far below them along the rocky foreshore, the sea was like a living thing, huge white capped waves rolling ever onwards east around the bottom of the earth, crashed and thundered along the entire western foreshore. While out to sea, here and there, dark ominous rain and snow squalls scudded quickly along the surface of the restless sea, trailing long streaky fingers of rain, sleet or snow in their wake.

"Up here on the wind-blown plateau, as they looked out over the restless sea they never gave their original home with all it electronic aids or comforts a single thought. Besides, at this moment they could see only one another, the future, and the warm cosy little honeymoon resort waiting for them back at Bauer Bay and no peeking spacecraft.

Apparently oblivious to the weather, a myriad of petrels, prions, shearwaters, Mother Carey's Chicken or Wilson's storm petrels dived and searched for food amongst the tumultuous waves. Sometimes, as they looked down upon the vast expanse of feather bed and tundra, they were often fortunate to see a great white wandering albatross returning after many weeks at sea to land with food for its offspring.

Like a magnificent white aircraft, they would come in against the wind, their incredibly large wings flapping and pumping down steadily, their giant tail fanned out and up acting like an air brake before dropping effortlessly onto the runway as though stepping onto a feathered cushion. As they watched, this great white bird would flap its wings and shake them out, carefully refold them and waddle gracefully over to the waiting chick with all the aloofness that is a Wandering Albatross.

Once back at Bauer Bay, with warm dry clothes on, after romantic candle light dinner, it was into their warm bed to snuggle up beneath the blankets and listen to the serenade of the roaring crashing hissing sea and the perpetual mournful howl of the ever-present wind… life it appeared, was just perfect. Unfortunately, for the happy couple, their week passed all too soon, it was already time to go.

As a new bride would soon want to decorate her own room here in this quiet retreat, Emma sadly packed her things and boxed up her personal linen and curtains. At last all set to go, it was one last look around, shouldering their large Carrymore backpack once more, they closed the door. Then gazing up the steep slope towards the distant plateau, they took a deep breath and headed out across the rippling laughing water still running madly out from under the featherbed and headed towards the overland track. North Head and whatever the future may hold.

Chapter 20
The Price of Power

"During those last few weeks of winter and into the early spring, the first new tower and turntable system for a wind-powered generator had been completed. As the daylight hours increased more and more, a work party carried the bags of cement, steel framework, nuts and bolts up to the western side of North Head above 'Catch me Point' and completed the tower. This spot was selected because of the continuous wind run and, as a power cable had to be run to it, its length relative to the station proximity was important.

"With the tower erected, a small work platform complete with a winch assembly was installed at the top. The turntable and alternator was hauled up onto North Head and installed. The cabling was terminated and run down to a control system and transformer at the base of the tower. Once the blades were fitted to the alternator, to stop them spinning, they were feathered and secured in a stationary position with a safety rope, then once everyone had evacuate the tower, the blades could be un-tethered and the work platform dismantled from below.

"Once the power cable was connected to the main buzz bars in the powerhouse, the rope would be removed and the blades moved electronically into course pitch and allowed to spin. Once up to generating speed normally 13-15 revolutions per minute, the pitch would be moved through into fine pitch and allowed to run constantly. The engines in the powerhouse could then be shut down thus saving precious fossil fuel stocks.

"With the tower completed, the alternator, propeller installed, Aub, one of the senior cadets in charge of the installation project was now dismantling the work platform, while changing his position under the platform, for some unknown reason he undone his safety harnesses and moved around the tower to his right. While stepping out and around one of his co-worker, there was a sudden strong just of wind, he missed his footing on the wet slippery steel framework and plunged twenty odd feet to the ground. While the thick tussock grass cushioned his fall, it unfortunately bounced him out over the edge of the plateau and in three or four stages fell several hundred feet to the rocks just north of 'Catch me Point'.

"As though in slow motion those still on the tower watched in horror as he went spinning and bouncing from ledge to ledge down the mountainside, to quickly disappear from sight. Stunned by what had just happened, the work party could only look at one another for a few moments in utter disbelief. While the wind, as quickly as it had sprung up had now abated, but the damage was done, as somewhere down the side of the mountain, Aub lay seriously injured or even dead. The remainder of the work party split up, some cautiously making their way down the steep tussock covered walls searching the mountainside, while one of the girls ran for home. Without any thought for her own safety, she scrambled quickly down the steep stairway cut into the south eastern wall of North Head to the isthmus below where gasping for breath; she staggered into the kitchen.

"'My God, Natalie what's wrong,' Mrs Moody asked the terrified girl.

"'It's Aub, he's gone over the side below the wind generator,' she gasped.

"Grabbing the telephone Mrs Moody rang the radio shack where Wayne raised the SAR alarm and every one assembled in the mess hall to listen as Natalie gasped out her story. The SAR team quickly swung into action, the stretcher and medical kit were brought out from the hospital, and along with the SAR crew equipped with ropes and climbing gear; they left the building and hurried towards the rocky western side of North Head.

"Down onto the western foreshore they ran, along the beach to 'Catch me Point', so called because it is a cave or tunnel open to the sea to the west under the cliff face and where you have to wait for the sea or the waves to recede before you make your way safely across the floor of the cave to the far side. Once you have achieved this, quickly climb up through the rock chimney or chute to the base of the cliff above. Today there was no waiting for the water to recede, the team simply plunged in and waded across against the swirling water to the far side. Once across, it was a simple matter of climbing up out of the cave through the chimney and followed the base of the cliff beneath North Head, to an area directly beneath the generator.

"Clinging precariously to the steep wall, other members of the work party could be seen cautiously making their way down the steep mountainside searching beneath the dense clumps of Tussock grass and Cabbage weed. But search as they may, there was no sign of Aub. It was apparent that he had gone all the way down to the rocks on the foreshore.

"A little further ahead of the SAR team, a frenzied flock of birds, namely giant petrels, Dominican gulls and skuas could be seen fluttering up out of the rocks or simply wheeling in out of the sky to land, led them to the spot where Aub lay. Knowing that these birds were carnivorous, the S.A.R party hurried as fast as they could across the rocky terrain where-to-their horror laid Aub. The birds were clustered around him and on him. They were drinking the small pools of blood forming around his body and picking at the loose pieces of flesh, which had been cut and torn from the exposed parts of his body during that horrendous fallen.

"Chasing the offending birds, Robbin checked his pulse and heaved a sigh of relief he was alive. From his position, it appeared that he had careered down the side of the mountain in several large bounces, each of thirty to forty feet apart, bouncing from one dense clump of tussock grass to the next finally coming to a stop, face down amongst the rocks. "Incredible as it may seem, although mortally injured and totally paralysed, he was still conscious.

"'Get them bloody birds off me,' he whispered.

"'It's okay mate, there gone now, we've got you now, just bloody hang in there, we are taking you home,' Robbin replied.

"With all the care they could muster, he was gently lifted and placed face down on the stretcher in a coma position, and once covered was strapped into position. As there was no way we could get the stretcher down the chimney or chute and into 'Catch me Cove' they would have to take him up onto the top of North Head and down the staircase to the station. Because he had lost a lot of blood and his blood pressure was very low, three blood transfusions were required at different levels on the way to the top of the North head. As the Doc wanted to be able to monitor him during the return trip to the station a pain-relieving drug was out of the question,

"Ropes lowered down the wall of North Head were attached to the leading edge of the stretcher to assist the six men supporting the stretcher above the tall grass. Then, with others by their side helped to lift and push the stretcher through the shoulder high cabbage weed, the long haul some 240 feet to the top of North Head commenced. Finally, some one and a half hours and three blood transfusions later, the sweating, exhausted SAR group crawled over the top of the cliff and handed the stretcher to fresh waiting helpers.

"Along the mountaintop, they hurried, down the slippery spiralling muddy stairway leading to the Isthmus far below and finally into the warm, re-assuring confines of the hospital. Here the emergencies trained for, yet procedures we prayed would never be required, swung into action. After cutting his tattered clothing off, he was scanned and x-rayed from head to foot, and the diagnosis was not good. His back was broken; both legs were dislocated ruptured at the knees where his legs had spun like propeller blades. His arms were broken, most ribs were broken, his legs were both broken and he was bleeding internally. Sadly, it would have been easier to list the few bones that were not broken! Other than that, as he would say, he was not in bad shape considering.

"The first thing to do was to stop the internal bleeding, so, as staff prepared him for the theatre everyone not directly connected with the running of the hospital was asked to leave and the medical team commenced its work. Dusk saw the abdominal operation on the vertical colon a success, the bleeding had been stopped and the blood pressure 125 over 85 had stabilise, while still in a serious state he not quite as critical as he was when he was first brought in. Robbin was worried as to how he could stabilise him further until something could be done with the multitude of injuries he had sustained. As any further movement would only aggravate his condition.

"Aub's girlfriend the other feral girl, Angie, stayed close by him holding his hand, not saying a word but watching everything like a hawk. She did not seem to understand why this strong young giant simply lay there sleeping, or like the child of nature she was, maybe she knew all right and nothing was going to shut her out.

"The whole community became involved in the all-out effort to save him. Some people made ice to pack around his body to lower the temperature. Others measure every drop of urine. His heart was monitor and scrutinised every minute to watch for the slightest waver. Temperature and constant blood pressure readings, the team fussed about him like a queen ant, while outside for some strange reason the space craft re-appeared and hovered silently above the hospital.

"In an effort to make the blood flow, Robbin sliced open his calf and quadriceps muscles to try to induce the blood to flow down into his critically injured legs, but to no avail. During that first long night as any wrong movement with his spine could kill him. Alvario made a wooden coffin like an ancient Egyptian coffin and once lined with padding and cotton wool he was carefully lifted up and set down into it to keep him stable. The damage to his legs was so bad, that in view of the fact that we did not have any vasco/cardiac expertise or a specialist to operate on the legs, repair the damage to the blood vessels, veins and arteries to regenerating the flow of blood to his lower legs; To save his life, they would both have to come off at the knees.

"This major under taking was fed into the surgical computer and relying on his strength to see him through and after several hours in the theatre, the operation was a success; once more, he came through the all right. Weeks went slowly by as all activities on the station were closed down to a bare minimum so that people were available to rally round the patient and the space craft had long since disappeared. With all this TLC, he seemed to be getting stronger, his knees were capped and he even discussed with Alvario the prospect of making a set of wooden legs like long John Silver so that he might tread once more the deck of the 'Polly Woodside'. So apart from the various broken bones, which would mend in time, the future looked a lot brighter.

"Then, one morning some eight weeks after his fall, Aub suddenly died!

"'What had happened?'

"'Why was he all right one minute and then suddenly dead?'

"The small close-knit community was in a state of shock, shattered; in a very short space of time this was their second brush with death and an uneasy feeling settled over the group. They were now even more conscious of the dangers these lush green walls were capable of.

"'But why?' That was the question.

"Robbin was at loss as to the reason.

"To find the answer an autopsy was conducted and it was found that he died of a brain clot.

"'Why would he die of a brain clot?'

"Once again that was an intriguing question, it did not simply just happen it must have been accidentally or deliberately caused? A coronial inquest into his death found that he had died of an accidental injection of Heparin. The Heparin had been used as a clotting agent and was introduced into the drip to coagulate the blood flow when his legs were amputated at the knees. Once the bleeding and the weeping stopped, and the flap of skin left there on each leg specifically to cap the injury was stitched to make a solid base on his upper legs, forming a non-sensitive area so false legs could be used, at which point the heparin was removed from the medication list.

"Someone on night duty some time prior to his death had apparently been reading his case history, noted the use of Heparin and without questioning why it was not being used, re-introduced it into the drip.

The tragic results we know.

An accident?

No names no pack drill.

"Yet, in fact we lost two people, for with the Aubrey untimely death, the spacecraft had re-appeared and after the subsequent burial in the little grave yard on North Head it disappeared and strange as may seem so did Angie. No one saw her leave the station and search as we may, over the coming years no trace of her or her body was ever found! With her man gone, it must have seemed to her, that there was nothing here for her to live for anymore. Could she have returned from whence she came, to the arm of Mother Nature by swimming out into the endless cold grey sea? Or…alternatively, did she voluntarily leave in a spacecraft?

Yet sometimes it seems that you can hear her singing a ballad that they both loved so well. Or was it just the sighing of the morning winds, which for some strange reason always seems to spring up just after dawn and as it passes up over North head, only ruffles the grass and wild native flowers that now grow in abundance on Aub's grave.

Yes…even in death, I think she comes back to claim what is rightfully hers!"

Chapter 21
The Station Exodus

"Throughout the remainder of that first year, as that first harsh winter had blown itself out and with the arrival of warm breeze of the coming spring, the memory of Aub's untimely departure slowly faded as the many weddings and that once in a lifetime excursion to Bauer Bay came and went.

"As the warmth of the Snow Fairy, the warm spring winds of the southern latitudes was felt across the land, winter's snow began to recede to the mountaintops and life on the island began anew. Emerging from the sea in their millions, king, royal, gentoo and rockhopper penguins once more popped from the raging surf hour after hour, day after day until it seemed the island was going to overflow. Lumbering up the beaches, hundreds of huge southern elephant seal beach masters emerged from the roaring surf to claim hereditary harem sites. There to fight all challengers for the right to lord over them; Once having established claim to such territory they then waited for the thousands of pregnant cows that would soon haul out to give birth, moult and mate before returning to the sea.

"The introduced flocks of sheep, herds of goats and Red Deer were also heavy with young and great care would have to be taken not to lose any new born out on the grazing slopes beneath the thick cover of cabbage weed and tussock grass. This initial success in reproducing the herds was a welcome relief to the community as it assured them of continuing supply of milk, butter, cheese and later as the herds increased fresh meat, wool and hides for leather.

"Also in the many hidden valleys, the lakes which had been seeded with hundreds of fingerlings, tell-tale rings on the surface of the once mirror flat waters suggested the fish had also proliferated and were feeding on surface lava. As the heavy sea swell of the past winter abated, the final deporting of heavy equipment and personal items to the various out-stations by sea began. The flocks were divided up and once herded up onto the plateau were driven south down the centre of the island. As the group passed each of the designated living quarters, the stock for that area was cut out and driven down the mountainside to the pens already constructed. The remainder would then move on to the next area until the herds were all delivered to their respective areas.

"Towards the end of summer, as one the group sat down to dinner for the last time and as this would be the last time they would ever sit down like this again, a sombre mood permeated Christmas day of 2153. They had been through so much together and had achieved so much over the past 18 months that they had become a close-knit family. Yet when this meal was finished, they would break up and depart for their own areas.

"The Caroline Cove and Hurd Point groups would take the Hover Craft to the west of the island, where after deporting at the far southwest corner of the island it would then continue on around the end of the Island to Hurd Point. While Green

Gorge and Lusitania Bay groups would take the Amphibian to the east, this way there would always be transport in case of emergency between each of those areas and in fact the main station. The groups leaving for Sandy Bay and Green Gorge (Red River area) would walk overland or along the coast.

"Finally, it was time to go and caught up in the excitement of the move the whole community milled about in the communal square. A hug here and a kiss there, then all too soon the engines of the hovercraft and the amphibian roared into life and once every one was safely aboard, they moved off. Down into the sea to the left and right of the isthmus, surging up over the waves and out to sea, they were soon lost from view in a cloud of sea spray.

"Those leaving on foot shouldered their backpacks and made their way down onto the beach and headed for the Nuggets, a prominent landmark which could be seen sticking out into the sea some three miles down the Eastern Sea board while en-route to Sandy Bay and Green Gorge.

"Apart from the Woof, woof, woofing of the blades of the wind generator on north head, the station was now strangely quiet; somehow, it did not seem the same without the exciting hustle and bustle of the past nine months. Ivan and Margaret, Tim and Margaret, Adrian and Sally and two young couples David and Emma and strange as it seemed both Natalie and her Will, and Lynda and her Matthew retired to the mess and had a cool drink of home-made beer to settle the nerves. The migration was a success and for the moment, the effort now told on the older members of the group.

"For them, it was a simple matter of removing sheets and returning it and other material to the clothing store. Finally closing up the rooms not being used. And as they would rely on the solar cells and the wind generator now whirring steadily away on North Head for power during the day light months, shutting down the engines, inhibiting and storing them for the future. Everything they had must now be conserved to the utmost, as God knows how long it would be until contact with the outside world was made even then would they want to migrate.

"The residents of North Head were now alone yet not alone; they had set up a new civilisation and in time a new generation would grow and live hand in hand with Mother Nature. They were responsible for the administration of the whole island in matters of health, policy, arbitration, administration and most importantly the preservation and maintenance of the Polly Woodside, the vessel that one-day may take a future generation back to Australia and what was once known as civilisation

"Like pages in a storybook, the seasons came and went so to the odd spacecraft. The first and second indigenous generation of Macquarie Islanders had been born. The first baby girl named 'Helene Maree' was born to Linda and Matthew and several new brides were now pregnant. As life continued, new leaders were elected and a whole new generation beyond tomorrow prospered. Having long since passed away, the original voyagers were now buried up here in this quiet little cemetery behind us on North Head.

"As the decades quickly passed measures that are more stringent were adopted to conserve what little they now had. Except in the winter, solar and wind generated power was used and solar powered heaters had been constructed to save burning the last few precious gallons of fossil fuel. Then one day out of the blue, it happened. Yes, although it was bound to happen sooner or later as the new generation had simply forgotten about the outside world, it came as quite a surprise. VKO-MI, VKO-MI, CQ CQ CQ; this is VK-COGG standing by!

"Fred the present leader at North Head simply stared in disbelief at the little slip of paper handed to him by the runner from the radio room, then rolling it up into a little ball, slid it into his pocket. That call sign was from their original home town. A city that this generation had only heard of in stories passed down from generation to generation."

Slowly the old man's voice faded to a whisper as though lost in the depth of time or carried out to sea on the sighing winds of the late afternoon.

"Grand Pa," Kathleen asked, "are you all right, Grand Pa?"

"Yes, love, I suppose I was just dreaming," the old man replied. "Well come on you lot," he said extending his hands. "Help me up," he chuckled, "your mothers will think I have got you all lost."

On their way back across the windy top of North Head, this fourth generation of children, waded happily through the vast fields of waving of tussock grass without as much as a glance in the direction of a civilisation they had only just heard about. Hand in hand as they passed the little white-fenced cemetery, a small piece of white paper fell from Grandpa's pocket and chased by the ever-present wind, went dancing across the top of the dense fields of grass to disappear out over the edge.

No one bothered to chase it:

Why…because it belonged to another world, a distant civilisation that was not theirs.

No, they were Macquarie Islander's; they were wild and free, the children of Mother Nature, which embraced them and knowing nowhere else, this was their home.

Making their way safely down the steep winding track to the living quarters far below, they happily ran for home. Yes, these were the children of a new generation…a generation 'Beyond Tomorrow'.

The End